D1321095

Port of Light

The Canary Islands are a Spanish possession but are much nearer to the coast of Africa than that of Spain. There has always been tension between the Islands and the Peninsula, and an official visit to them by the President of the Council of Ministers is more than a little fraught. That is why Superintendent Bernal of the Madrid CID and his team are despatched to Grand Canary to monitor the local criminal and political situation independent of the President's own bodyguard.

The move suits Bernal, whose mistress Consuelo Lozano has discreetly got her bank to post her to Las Palmas, capital of Grand Canary, to await the birth of their child. Now Bernal will be able to be with her for the birth—except that she fails to meet him at the airport as arranged.

Torn between anxiety for Consuelo, who has been kidnapped by unknowns and spirited away to the mountainous interior of the island, and the need to make sense of a series of sinister events beginning with the murder of a blind lottery-ticket seller, Bernal has his work cut out to ensure the President's safety and that of his beloved, for the two are closely linked.

DAVID SERAFÍN

Port of Light

A Superintendent Bernal novel

COLLINS, 8 GRAFTON STREET, LONDON W1

William Collins Sons & Co. Ltd
London · Glasgow · Sydney · Auckland
Toronto · Johannesburg

First published 1987
© David Serafín Ltd 1987

British Library Cataloguing in Publication Data

Serafín, David
    Port of light.—(Crime Club)
    I. Title
    823'.914[F]   PR6069.E7/

    ISBN 0 00 232114 9

Photoset in Linotron Baskerville by
Rowland Phototypesetting Ltd
Bury St Edmunds, Suffolk
Printed in Great Britain by
William Collins Sons & Co. Ltd, Glasgow

For Dorothy and Lynn, remembering
the MV *Monte Umbe*.

Author's note: The setting is Madrid and Las Palmas in July
1982, but the events and personages described are entirely
fictitious.

D.S.

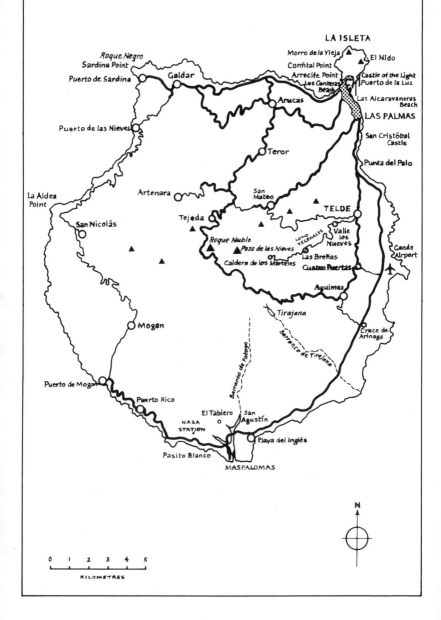

GRAND CANARY

LA ISLETA
Morro de la Vieja
El Nido
Confital Point
Arrecife Point
Castle of the Light
Las Canteras Beach
Puerto de la Luz
Las Alcaravaneras Beach
LAS PALMAS

Roque Negro
Sardina Point
Puerto de Sardina
Galdar
Arucas

Puerto de las Nieves

San Cristóbal Castle

Punta del Palo

Teror

La Aldea Point

Artenara
San Mateo
TELDE

Tejeda
Valle los Nueves
Gando Airport

Roque Nublo
LOMO TEGENALES
△ Pozo de las Nieves
Las Breñas
San Nicolás
Caldera de los Marteles
Cuatro Puertas

Agüimes

Mogan
Tirajana

Cruce de Arinaga

Puerto de Mogan
Barranco de Fataga
Barranco de Tirajana

Puerto Rico
El Tablero
San Agustín
NASA STATION
Playa del Inglés
Pasito Blanco
MASPALOMAS

N

0 1 2 3 4 5
KILOMETRES

Gregorio *el lotero* sold his last lottery ticket of the day, quite unexpectedly, in the Aquí Te Espero Bar opposite the entrance to the Las Palmas passenger-liner dock. Unexpectedly, because the oddly named bar was normally frequented by foreign seamen who were never interested in buying a daily lottery ticket, for, in the unlikely event of winning, they would suffer the inconvenience of a trip to the office of the Delegación in the city centre to collect the prize between 10.0 a.m. and 1.0 p.m. the following day.

Most of them had never ventured further along the isthmus from the port than the Plaza de Santa Catalina, the square in front of the town quay that formed the natural meeting-place of seafarers, traders, drug-pushers, prostitutes and the foreign tourists who were hoping for a not too dangerous thrill.

He wondered if the Aquí Te Espero—'Here I Wait For You'—had got its name from the whores of all shapes and nationalities who sat on tiny wooden swings suspended from the high ceiling by thick hawsers, oscillating drunkenly as they forlornly awaited the return of fondly remembered clients. Uttering low obscenities, they pushed rudely at Gregorio *el lotero* as he made his way to the street, tightly clutching the inner pocket of his worn and shiny waistcoat where he guarded the evening's takings. He would hand the money in at the branch office in the Calle de Juan Rejón on his way home, he thought; safer than carrying it all back through the emptying streets of El Refugio—that narrow stretch of land which the sea once covered at high water, where the first settlers of Gran Canaria used to take refuge from the attacks of the fierce aborigines.

After handing over his takings and obtaining the official

receipt, Gregorio tapped his way past the Castle of the Light, whence came the heavy clonking noise of the bowls thrown by the *boliche* players in the palm-fronded park opposite, and the subsequent cries of delight or chagrin as someone's *bocha* was knocked far away from the jack. The familiar sound warned him he had reached the entrance to the Calle de Gordillo, which led steeply up to La Isleta, the last and poorest outpost of Las Palmas, where his wife would be preparing their evening *potaje* of watercress or cabbage leaves. The air touched his face with a warm thickness that seemed to rise bodily from the harbour after darkness fell, and he could sense its density even as he moved the point of his light-wood cane from side to side in a rapid snakeshead rhythm.

Gregorio *el lotero* listened to the various sounds and sniffed the distinctive smells, all of which were familiar and orientating, and he smiled at the soft wailing voice of José Vélez, the island's most popular singer, which emerged from a jukebox turned up loud in a bar, proclaiming, a little unnecessarily, in a heavy Canaries accent: *'Él me yama canarito porque yo nasí en Canarias*—He calls me the little canary because I was born in the Canaries.'

Gregorio groped at the now empty metal clip at his lapel with some satisfaction: fifty *tiras* sold at 250 pesetas each, which, at a commission of ten per cent, had given him 1250 pesetas profit for the day—much more than his wife would have earned from the laundry she took in. This was quite a remarkable take for a Tuesday, when people were feeling the pinch before their next payday.

As the street got steeper, rising towards the peak of La Isleta—The Little Island—which was the most nor'-easterly point of the Grand Canary, the intermittent beam of the lighthouse cut across the oily waters of Las Canteras Bay and swept on, over the rooftops and the bare volcanic crags above, extending more dimly to the masts in the harbour on the eastern side, where it competed with the rippling line of smoky moonlight coming in from the African Sea.

Gregorio *el lotero* noted almost automatically the ten side-streets he had to cross, stopping at each pavement edge and feeling for the kerb on the other side with his darting stick. As he was approaching the last corner, where he would turn into the Calle del Coronel Rocha, he suddenly pricked up his ears at an unusual sound emanating from one of the houses on the left. His wife had told him that these dwellings were now derelict and she had speculated on whether they might be able to afford to rent one of them and do it up—it would certainly be larger than the flat-roofed two-roomed hovel in which they now lived.

After crossing the street, Gregorio stopped to listen again: the noise was definitely louder, and resembled the angry buzz of a wasp, but that it was electronic in origin he had no doubt. He could also hear a high-pitched oscillation and the noise of radio static, followed by the rapid chatter of Morse. That's strange, he thought; it doesn't sound like the walkie-talkies of the police. He was used to hearing those, both from passing police cars and from the *guardias* on their beat. Perhaps it was something to do with the coastguard station; but that was much higher up, perched on the dark volcanic rock above the last of the hovels.

Far below, to the north-west, Gregorio could hear the waves breaking over La Barra—the long bar of sharp rocks that protected the Playa de las Canteras from the Atlantic current. Suddenly the loud buzzing stopped, and the clacking of the Morse key started up again, very close to where he was standing. His curiosity overcoming his hesitance, the blind man turned into the open doorway of the abandoned house.

'Who's there? What are you doing?' he called out.

Inspector Guedes of the Las Palmas Judicial Police, who was in charge of the Miller Bajo *comisaría,* was called to the foot of the rocks below the Isleta lighthouse at 6.35 a.m. the next day, Wednesday 7 July. The body had been spotted soon after first light by a pair of Civil Guards attached to the Marine Division, and it was urgent for it to be photographed and its position carefully noted before high water, due at 11.33 a.m. Guedes could see at once that it was going to be difficult to recover: it lay well beyond reach from the rocks, half-submerged in the still waters inside the protection of La Barra, where it was caught on a small projection too near to the rocky bar for a boat to approach in safety.

He offered his packet of Winston to the Civil Guards as they waited for the police surgeon, the forensic technician and the judge of instruction.

'Do you think it's a floater, washed ashore from a ship?' Guedes asked the older of the civil guards.

'Possibly, sir. Last night's high water was at twelve-fifteen, and all these rocks are covered then. The height of tide is about two and a half metres at this time of year. When the tide ebbed, the corpse would naturally get trapped by the bar. It could have come from a passing vessel.'

Guedes sighed. 'That will give us a lot of work, with about thirty sailings and arrivals every day and half that number at each high tide. But if the dead man was a crewman who fell overboard when drunk, there's a good chance that the captain of the vessel will get in touch with the port authorities by radio when he discovers him missing. I'll ring the harbour-master and find out which ships sailed in or out in a north-westerly direction round Confital Point last night.'

'All the ferries to Tenerife sail past here, Inspector,' the older coastguard pointed out. 'He could have fallen off one of those. And it depends how long he's been in the water.'

Guedes borrowed the Civil Guard's powerful 30 × 70 binoculars and trained them on the partly sunken corpse.

'Many hours by the look of it.'

He focused the heavy Japanese prismatics on to the head of the cadaver, which floated face up, mostly submerged from the waist downwards.

'The fish have been at him a bit. The eyes and mouth mainly.' He adjusted the focusing-wheel more precisely. 'There's a deep diagonal gash across the forehead. Could he have been caught by a propeller, perhaps?'

Guedes handed the binoculars back to the Civil Guard as he observed two cars and a mortuary van approaching along the stony track.

'Here they come now. We'd better arrange for a launch to be brought round.'

'I think a flat-bottomed rowing-boat would be more useful, sir,' said the younger coastguard timidly. 'A boat with any draught would get torn apart on those rocks. The tide's turned now, but it'll be some hours before a launch could get safely over the bar, and we might lose the body in the undertow before then.'

'Very well. I'll radio in for a sturdy dinghy to be brought across by trailer. You two are experienced rowers, I take it?'

'My father was a fisherman out of Puerto de la Luz, sir,' said the older guard. 'We'll manage OK, but we'll need grappling-hooks as well.'

'Good, I'll get them sent over. I'd better go and greet the judge of instruction.'

As he switched off his car radio after calling Central Control, Inspector Guedes observed two men of the Policía Nacional—the name newly given to the force by the post-Franco democratic Government—get out of the first large SEAT saloon, adjust their smart new beige and brown uniforms and place their brown berets at a more jaunty angle before saluting the judge as he alighted from a dark blue Mercedes.

Judge Velasco descended gravely, touching his black broad-banded and wide-brimmed hat to the uniformed men, and proceeded in a careful and dignified walk towards Guedes, who reflected that the judge's dress was not only practical in its complete sobriety, but also traditional in the Islands, where the elders had always favoured a black

Sunday garb for all formal, and most informal, occasions. And he looked born to the role: close-cropped, curly black hair, grizzled at the sides, a sallow and heavily wrinkled face with sad, expressive eyes and the long face and large jaw of the *guanches*—more properly the name of the aboriginal tribe of Tenerife, but extended loosely to include the native inhabitants of Gran Canaria too.

'*Buenos días, señor juez.* It seems we have a "floater" from a passing ship, caught on the rocks of La Barra.'

One of the coastguards offered his binoculars to the judge, who gently brushed them aside.

'An awkward one to get at, Inspector. You're certain it's the body of a man?' The judge screwed up his eyes in peasant fashion under his thick, white-flecked brows.

'I don't think there's any doubt, sir, judging by the short hair and the stubble on the chin. And he's wearing an old-fashioned shirt buttoned up to the neck and what appear to be a dark waistcoat and trousers.'

'If he's fallen off a ship, would a seaman be dressed like that?'

The old judge was shrewd, thought Guedes, despite the lack of attentiveness suggested by his almost Oriental inscrutability.

'How would he have got that wound on the forehead?'

The inspector was quite stunned by this incontrovertible evidence of the judge's lynx-like vision, remarkable in a man in his early seventies at least.

'The propeller of a vessel, sir?' he put forward tentatively.

'H'm, could be. But what about the clothing, eh?'

'Most of the inter-island ferries pass the point near here, sir. He could have fallen off one of them last night in the darkness, without anyone noticing.'

'Or have been pushed off, eh?'

Guedes was not unaware that this judge had something of a reputation for being over-suspicious, and had been known to ferret away at the most straightforward case to see if anything was being covered up. Guedes now felt he should assert himself as investigating officer.

'We'll let the pathologist see him first, if that meets with your approval, sir. In the meantime I'll be contacting the harbour-master and via him the masters of the vessels that sailed or docked yesterday and in the early hours of this morning.'

'Very well, Guedes. How are you proposing to recover the body?'

'I've sent for a dinghy to be brought by trailer, sir. I don't think we'd get a launch over the bar safely before high water.'

The judge pulled out a loosely-rolled Canary cheroot from his top pocket and bit off the end before lighting it. He glanced again at the corpse which was bobbing gently in the swell a hundred metres or so away, and let his gaze move slowly across the rocky shoreline that rose steeply towards the Punta de Arrecife and the dirty brown peak of La Isleta.

'Don't neglect the Missing Persons' List, Guedes, once you find out the approximate time of immersion from the pathologist's report.'

On the morning of Tuesday 6 July, a secret meeting had been scheduled to take place in the Seed House of the Moncloa Palace in Madrid at 9.0 a.m. The President of the Council of Ministers' private secretary checked to see if the conference table was set out properly for the eight people who would be attending. Satisfied with the lay-out, he unrolled a wall-map of the Canaries Archipelago at the farther end of the elegantly furnished room, the windows of which offered a splendid view of the park that sloped westwards to the River Manzanares, now reduced to a trickle by the very hot July weather.

Soon the secretary heard the sentries drawing to attention as the Vice-President arrived, accompanied by the Civil Governors of the two Canaries Provinces who had flown in the previous evening from El Gando and Los Rodeos airports respectively. The secretary looked at his watch as he went out to the vestibule to greet the newcomers: it was 8.55 a.m. No sooner had the main door been shut when it was re-opened for the Sub-Secretary of the Interior Ministry and the Captain-General of the Canaries military region, who had been driven up in official limousines. On the stroke of nine, they were joined by the Head of the President's personal bodyguard.

When they had all assembled, the Vice-President took the chair and invited the Head of Security to begin the proceedings.

'We are here, gentlemen, to finalize the plans for the President's visit to the Canaries from the fourteenth to the eighteenth of this month. In front of you, you will find a copy of the proposed itinerary, together with details of the official engagements and stopping places.'

'Before we go any further, Comisario,' said the Vice-President, 'perhaps we should ask the Captain-General and the Civil Governors to comment on the current political climate in the Archipelago, and the principal dangers to the President's security.'

The two Civil Governors looked at each other and at the Captain-General, then the Tenerife-based civil chief began to speak first.

'Things are pretty quiet at the moment in my province, apart from occasional brushes between the military *godos* and the locals.' He looked somewhat accusingly at the Captain-General as he used the Canaries slang word for those who came to boss them from the Peninsula: 'the Goths'. The army chief started to flush with anger, and the Civil Governor hurried on in his soft *tinerfeño* accent: 'The principal extremist group is, of course, the MPAIAC, which seeks full independence, with Polisario and Algerian assistance. But most of its activists are in exile and we keep a close watch on the young recruits who remain. Their main activity is distributing clandestine leaflets of a decidedly Marxist-Leninist slant.

But I don't think they'll present any threat to the President during his visit.'

'Perhaps you should get the police to round them up just before the President arrives,' commented the Captain-General. 'It's always better to be on the safe side with that *canalla*.' He glared at the Civil Governor.

'The President would prefer you not to do that,' said the Vice-President hastily. 'The general election is due in October and we don't want to cause any more ill-feeling than we can help. This is meant to be a vote-raising operation. What about the President's itinerary in Tenerife? Is that all right?'

The Civil Governor of that westerly group of islands looked at the typewritten summary with care. 'On the whole I think it's safer for the President to fly in at the new Queen Sofía airport in the south of the island rather than the old Los Rodeos one, which is commonly fogbound, although this will mean a much longer car drive to El Puerto de la Cruz, where he is scheduled to make his first speech. Naturally we'll take the usual precautions along the route.'

'Couldn't a helicopter be used to fly him from the Queen Sofía to El Puerto?' asked the Vice-President.

'It could be, but the machines aren't really very safe on the island,' commented the Captain-General. 'There are strong down-draughts from the peak of El Teide from the north-east trades and turbulence from the contrary inshore breeze; the air temperature can vary suddenly by eight to ten degrees in a hundred metres and we've lost quite a few choppers there over the years.' He sounded rather cheerful at the prospect, as though he wouldn't mind losing another containing the ineffectual President.

'One must balance the dangers in either case,' said the chief of the President's bodyguard. 'The car trip from the new airport on the new TF-21 highway will be much longer, but safer. There are fewer places where an ambush could be mounted. I've gone over the ground myself.'

'What about the day trip to La Gomera island?' asked the Vice-President. 'Must that be done by the local ferry?'

'It's certainly safer than a speedboat or one of your choppers,' said the chief of the bodyguard to the Captain-General, 'but again much slower.'

'We've arranged an official luncheon on board for the local party chiefs,' said the Tenerife civil governor, 'and the GEAs will check the ship for limpet-mines and bombs early that morning.'

'The Navy will also put an electronic screen around the ship from two submarines,' commented the Captain-General. 'No terrorist commandos could get through that undetected.'

'Let's hope the sea won't be choppy,' remarked the Vice-President; 'the President isn't a very good sailor.'

'He'll be well guarded in the hotel complex at El Puerto the first night,' commented the Civil Governor, 'and he'll spend the second night, after the La Gomera trip, in the official residence in Santa Cruz with me. He'll be completely secure there.'

'There is a further matter, before we look at the arrangements for Gran Canaria and Fuerteventura,' said the Vice-President. 'The President's security advisers are concerned about the comparative lack of senior officers in the police brigades both in Las Palmas and Tenerife. What I'm really asking you is whether we ought not to send out some experienced officers of assistant superintendent rank or above to reinforce the local brigades during the presidential visit.' He looked at the two Civil Governors expectantly.

The Governor of Tenerife province returned his gaze coolly. 'I think it could cause some resentment among our own people, who have been complaining for some time about their poor promotion prospects. And there's no actual cause for alarm, is there, Mr Vice-President?'

The Civil Governor of Gran Canaria hastened to concur

with his colleague on this point, though they did not always see eye to eye on all matters.

'Very well, gentlemen. But if anything crops up between now and the start of the visit, I shall want this proposal to be reconsidered. I have asked to be informed immediately by the Servicios de Información of anything out of the ordinary detected in your islands.'

On the evening of that same scorching July Tuesday in Madrid, Superintendent Luis Bernal was browsing at the bookstalls that backed on to the Botanical Gardens in the Cuesta de Claudio Moyano. As usual, he was searching for reasonably priced copies of books on old Madrid to add to his not inconsiderable collection. How cheap books used to be on the higgledy-piggledy shelves of the thirty-odd faded grey sheds that housed the street-booksellers.

He wasn't old enough to remember the perambulatory book-vendors who had caused traffic jams by trundling their carts along the Paseo del Prado in the early Twenties until they had been forcibly removed by the mayor, who had offered them this hill running from Retiro Park to Atocha railway station as a permanent home, but Bernal had seen old photographs of the street scenes of that period. Now in the 1980s many of the stall-holders had forsaken antiquarian and second-hand books in favour of what Bernal regarded as *basura*—rubbishy paperbacks whose contents, badly translated from no doubt execrable American English, surely could not betray the dubious promise of their lurid covers. Yet there were still three or four *tenderetes* where the aged proprietors maintained the more honourable tradition but at prices he regarded as staggering; they knew him, of course, as a regular and valued customer and usually lowered the touristic price marked inside the cover of a particularly choice item.

Today Bernal felt at peace with the world, at least with his particular bit of it. He had taken three days' leave after his

most recent homicide case, although he had spent much of
the time in his second, secret apartment writing up the legal
reports for the magistrate of Juzgado No. 16 who was to hear
the deposition the following day. Bernal still felt obliged to
make his way home as ever to his wife Eugenia for the
evening meal and an uneasy night's rest at her prayerful
side—the uneasiness deriving mainly from the supper of
warmed-up leftovers she customarily prepared.

By a quarter to eight, his eyes had tired of scanning the
rows of dusty books as he pushed his way through the throng
of students and bibliophiles of all ages; he decided to cross
the Calle de Alfonso XII and enter the Retiro Park through
the Gate of the Fallen Angel in order to stroll home in the
comparative coolness under the trees. After passing the
open space near the lake where children were trying out
their radio-controlled model aeroplanes, he made for the
O'Donnell exit and decided to reward himself for this exer-
cise with a Larios *gin-tonic* in Félix Pérez's bar. Once in the
street, he checked his loose change to see if he had enough to
call his mistress Consuelo Lozano, who was in Las Palmas
expecting their first child. He couldn't risk letting Eugenia
overhear the conversation if he rang from home, although he
had good grounds for suspecting that she had become aware
that he had formed this deep attachment outside their dismal
marriage, which had in a real sense broken down more than
eighteen years before.

Bernal entered one of the new interurban and international telephone kiosks outside the Escuela de Aguirre and
checked his watch to make sure it was past 8.0 p.m. when the
cheaper rate came into operation. He consulted his pocket-
book for the Las Palmas prefix and dialled the number. He
expected Consuelo to be home from the bank long since, even
though the Canaries were an hour behind the Peninsula. He
heard a series of clicks and then the long intervals of the
ringing tone. At last the phone was answered by a girl who
spoke in a thick Canaries accent.

'*Sí, diga.*'

'*Oiga, señorita.* Is Señora Lozano there?' Bernal recognized the voice as that of the servant Consuelo had hired.

'Who wants her?' asked the girl.

'This is her husband.' He and Consuelo had agreed that during the six months she would spend seconded to the branch of the Banco Ibérico in the Canaries she would pass herself off as a married woman whose husband was kept in Madrid by his work.

'*Ah, buenas tardes, Señor Lozano.*' The girl had clearly formed the mistaken impression that Lozano was Conchi's married surname. 'The Señora went to the bank as usual this morning but she hasn't come back yet. She said she'd be doing some shopping this afternoon for more things for the baby's layette ready for when it arrives in ten days' time. She's expecting you here before then.'

'I'm hoping to get away soon. Will you tell her that I'll try to ring her again later tonight?'

'*Sí, señor, con mucho gusto. Hasta luego.*'

Bernal was mildly surprised that Consuelo, who was due to give birth (much to her socialist chagrin) on 18 July, the anniversary of Franco's uprising against the Second Republic, should have had such a long day out, but there was no telling how women in the last stages of pregnancy might react; he remembered that Eugenia had once gone barefoot on a pilgrimage to the shrine of Our Lady of Guadalupe before giving birth to their first son Santiago, just to pray for an easy delivery.

Bernal turned at last into his favourite old bar in the Calle de Alcalá, where the barman was pouring out his gin and tonic in anticipation of his order, and then offered him a canapé of *bonito* paste. Don Félix, the old proprietor who was now semi-retired, came over to chat with him and to reminisce about the time he had played in the national team with Santiago Bernabeu at Wembley Stadium in 1924. Don Félix's father had been postmaster to King Alfonso XIII and after the fall of the monarchy in 1931 had taken over this ancient establishment in the Calle de Alcalá, with its tiny false gallery over the entrance to the back room where the locals played *tute* and *mus* on green baize-topped cardtables. Bernal knew that Don Félix approved of him, not only because he was a police superintendent but because he always wore a tie, which was regarded there as the mark of a gentleman.

After taking his leave by shaking hands with the upright eighty-year-old ex-footballer and turning into his own street, still putting off the unprodigal return to Eugenia's tender mercies, Bernal stopped to chat with the hall porter's sister, Doña Pilar, who remarked on the unbearable heat of the day, the constant hammering of the workmen repairing the burst pipe on the fifth floor, the scandalous behaviour of the woman on the third left front apartment, who called herself a widow and was no better than she ought to be, the stench of the refuse dropped by the dustmen each morning on the staircase which she had to pick up on her hands and knees, the outrageous dress, manners and behaviour of young people in general, especially the girls whose language was worse than troopers', the slowness of the Ayuntamiento in repairing the street outside which had been dug up for over a year now, and finally the terrifying crime wave since the Caudillo had departed this life—wasn't it a miracle that they weren't all murdered in their beds by the GRAPOs or the *etarras* or some newer brand of terrorists? And the deputies sitting on their *poltronas* in the Cortes drinking coffee and even stronger beverages most probably, discussing the bringing back of divorce and abortion, which would signify the end of society as they knew it, and hadn't the late Generalísimo been all too right when he'd said *No os puedo dejar solos*—You can't be left to yourselves?

Bernal found this litany of grievances only slightly more vocal than his wife's idea of small talk and he'd long developed the knack of letting it flow over him while making suitable facial reactions of ever-increasing concern, disquiet and alarm, which seemed to be all that the interlocutress required. Finally managing to close the doors of the elegant but rickety Isabelline lift, while the plaintive tones of the portress grew shriller through the open upper half of the lodge door, Bernal began to ascend uncertainly through the gloomy well of the staircase, unconsciously identifying the cooking smells of the dinners being prepared on each of the floors below his own.

He found the flat in darkness, with Eugenia seated in one of the uncomfortable rexine-covered armchairs reciting her black-beaded rosary. She reached the end of an *Ave Maria* and pointed sharply to a note left on the small round dining-table.

'They've been calling you all day. Where have you been?' she asked accusingly. 'The Minister wants to speak with you.'

'The Minister?' he asked in some surprise.

'Yes, he rang in person to invite you to dine with him tonight at a restaurant in Chamberí. I've written down the name of it.'

'Where's Diego? Isn't he in yet?'

'Been and gone,' she said sharply. 'He never does any studying. If only he were like his elder brother,' she moaned. 'Those fees we're paying for him at the University of Santiago are money down the drain. You ought to put your foot down and make him study, or else leave off and find a job to earn his own living. No moral fibre, that's what's wrong with him. And all the times I've taken him to Mass and confession, and even for special instruction from Father Anselmo. But it's no good. Bad blood will out, and it's not from my side of the family,' she ended pointedly.

By 11.0 a.m. on Wednesday 7 July in Las Palmas, Inspector Guedes watched the police pathologist sew up the remains of the 'floater'.

'You'll have my preliminary report typed up by late this afternoon, Inspector. But I can't tell you much about the cause of death until the organs have been analysed. The gash on the forehead could have occurred just before death, judging by the incipient vital signs at the edges of the wound, but it can't have been caused by the propeller of a boat, in my opinion. Something blunter, I think. The end of the instrument was rounded.' He pointed to the place on the bloated and unrecognizable face of the deceased lying on the white marble slab. 'The marine creatures have attacked the orifices unprotected by the clothing.'

'How long has he been in the water?' Guedes asked.

'Some twelve to fifteen hours I estimate from the state of the epidermis. Note the development of washerwoman's skin on the fingers and palms. You'll want fingerprints, if I can take them, to make the ID? I'll have to remove the skin and mount each fingertip on wax, because the wrinkling makes it impossible to take them direct.'

'Do you think he could have been attacked on a ship and then pushed overboard?'

'There is a fair amount of water in the lungs and pinpoints of petechiæ there, so I'm pretty sure he died of drowning and not from the contusion on the head. But we'd better wait for the analyses. I can't see any other cause of death. He was quite healthy for his age.'

'What would you put it at, Doctor?' asked Guedes.

'Mid-fifties, I'd say. Curious callouses on his right palm, but none on his left. Also he was flat-footed; must have walked a lot in his employment. There is an interesting pair of two small holes regularly placed in the left breast-pocket of his waistcoat. Could he have worn a badge of some kind which has fallen out?'

'You're surely not suggesting he was a policeman!' commented Guedes, who picked up the garment from the pile of clothing to examine it. 'He was poorly dressed, wouldn't you say, but not the common garb of a seaman necessarily. The

white plimsolls are badly worn and their soles are heavily
indented on the instep as though he walked with the feet
more widely splayed than the norm.'

'Don't the contents of the pockets give you any clues,
Inspector?' asked the doctor, who was sewing up the long
incision he had made in the abdomen and torso. 'There was a
lot of loose change in the right trouser-pocket, four hundred
and fifty-five pesetas' worth. Much more than the average
person would carry. The weight of it turned the body side-
ways and lowered its floating position. Could he have been a
barman on a ship?'

'But he would have been much more elegantly dressed in
that case,' said Guedes.

Bernal entered The Old Colonial with some trepidation. His
own social background still made him feel awkward in very
swish surroundings where he felt he lacked the easy grace
shown by those who had never known what it was like to
wonder where the next meal would come from. The ornate
green door with its heavy brass fittings, the lack of a sign
announcing the entrance to the famous restaurant, the
assumption that the prospective diners would not need to see
the price of the menu before entering and would simply know
that they were to press the discreet bellpush to gain admit-
tance (with the corollary that those who didn't spot the bell
wouldn't be welcome in any case); the feeling that it was a
grand private house which one was privileged to enter, a club
for the crème de la crème of eaters and eaten, gave Bernal
reason to pause on the threshold.

As though sensing his uncertainty, the courteous owner
swung open the well-oiled door at that very moment and
with a knowing naturalness, as though between equals in
wealth and power, said smoothly: 'Good evening. Superintendent Bernal, isn't it? The Minister is waiting for you in
the salon.'

That gentleman was exquisitely dressed in a suit probably

tailored for him in Savile Row, thought Bernal, as he was shaken warmly by the hand and led to a table set in a discreet bay flanked by two basketwork chairs with tall backs shaped like fans.

'I'm so pleased you could come for this small *tête-à-tête* dinner, Comisario. What would you like to drink?'

'I'm honoured to be invited, Minister. A gin and tonic, I think.'

The attentive proprietor in person soon brought them two immense apéritif glasses rimed with ice and topped by what appeared to be a considerable fruit salad.

'I'll come to the point at once, Comisario, so that we can go on to enjoy our meal,' the Minister began, lighting up a thin Havanna cheroot. 'Next week the President is going on a five-day tour of the Canary Islands to meet the party workers in each major centre and to address two rallies, one in Santa Cruz de Tenerife and the other in Las Palmas. I'm concerned with his personal security. His own bodyguard will be taking the usual precautions and the local civil governors are cooperating fully, of course. But still I'm somewhat uneasy about the visit. The Islands have been stirred up for some time, first by the MPAIAC—the independence movement headed by Cubillo, who as you know took refuge in Algiers —and more recently the young Marxist-Leninist groups. And they're finding supporters: despite the continuing free-port status and the low ten-per-cent tariff on imports, their economy is in a mess. There's been a great influx of Asian traders, who form almost a Mafia in the ports and tourist centres, and there are the usual disputes among the old *caciques* over control of the water supplies. But none of this is of prime importance for this visit.' The Minister paused to take a generous draught on his gin and tonic. 'The real destabilization started in 1975 with the Saharan "Green March" and our formal handing over of the Spanish Sahara to Morocco and Mauritania in February 1976. The Polisario Front is what worries me. You realize they are demanding the return, as they put it, of the Archipelago to mainland Africa? It's an absurd idea, of course, since the islands have never been African racially or in any other sense despite their geographical proximity to El Aaiún.'

Bernal began to wonder where he was to figure in all this and looked expectantly at the Minister, who was nibbling a salmon canapé.

'I propose to send two teams, one to Tenerife and the other to Gran Canaria, a week before the President arrives, to work with the local police but independently of the President's own security men. Their task will be to examine the local criminal and political situation and monitor it right to the end of the President's visit. Now I've checked with the Sub-Secretary of the Interior and the Head of the Brigada Criminal and they assure me that you and your group could be seconded at the present time. I also propose to send Zurdo and his group; you've heard that he has just been promoted to the rank of assistant superintendent?'

'Yes, and I'm delighted for him. We've worked together on a number of cases in the past.'

'So I understand. That's why I chose him, because you'll need to cooperate fully at all times. You'll both have to tread delicately with the local authorities, who will resent your presence.'

'How exactly do you envisage our work there, Minister? Have you or the CESID anything concrete for us to investigate?'

'Not really, Bernal. In the last couple of years you've been involved in far-reaching political cases which you've resolved most satisfactorily. I simply want you to take your team out there and get the feel of the place, to examine the most recent criminal reports and the detailed local political information, especially about extremists of all kinds. It's always so much better to have a group in place at least a week before an official visit to take the temperature of the water, as it were.'

Bernal pondered on the vagueness of the proposed operation, but realized that it would provide him with a golden
opportunity to be at Consuelo's side during the birth of their
child, so he decided to grasp the bull by the horns.

'Very well, Minister. I'll gather my team together and
we'll get out there right away. I'd be grateful if you
could allot us to Gran Canaria, which I know better than
Tenerife.'

'Excellent, Bernal. Just as you wish. I'm sure Zurdo will
be happy to take his group to Santa Cruz de Tenerife. You'll
both have full Presidential authority. I suggest that the two
of you have a briefing meeting with the Sub-Secretary of the
Interior before you leave. We'll ensure that you have the
power to overrule all other police forces and military authority other than the CESID and the President's personal
bodyguard.' The Minister turned to the exotic menu with a
sigh of satisfaction. 'Now perhaps you'd like to select
your starter and main course. How about some lobster
Thermidor?'

Bernal gloomily perused the list with increasing gastric
tension, hoping to find some dish less aggressive to the
battered lining of his long-suffering stomach.

The wife of Gregorio *el lotero*, ever more worried by her
husband's failure to arrive home by 11.0 p.m. on the sixth,
had resolved to go out and search for him. She had turned off
the old butane-gas stove some hours earlier to allow the
cabbage stew to cool. Surely he hadn't got drunk in one of the
many bars he visited, or fallen down somewhere as a con-
sequence of the many *chatos* of white wine his acquaintances
had treated him to? She hoped that at least he'd paid in the
lottery money at the ONCE branch office.

She put on a stained blue woollen cardigan and closed the
outer door of their two-roomed dwelling without locking it;
after all, what was there to steal? She emerged into the dark,
deserted street where she could glimpse the harbour lights

far below. As she made her way down the steep hill, her face was illuminated from time to time by the intermittent beam from the lighthouse at El Puerto de la Luz. The shabbily dressed woman reached the first of the cheap bars and somewhat nervously pushed aside the beaded curtain that hung over the entrance; she was so little accustomed to entering bars or cafés that she felt as though she were walking on to a theatrical stage. Fortunately there was no one there other than the barman, who was wiping glasses at the far end of the bar and she knew him by sight.

'Have you seen my husband?' she asked diffidently.

'That would be Gregorio the blind man, wouldn't it?'

'Yes, that's right. You see, he hasn't come home to supper as he usually does at half past nine. I'm afraid he's had a fall or some kind of accident.'

'Well, he hasn't been in here today, unless he was here this morning when the boss looks after things.'

'Thanks all the same. I'd better look in at all the bars between here and the branch office of the ONCE,' she sighed.

The owner of the next bar she tried said he thought he'd heard the tapping of Gregorio's stick as he passed up the hill about two hours earlier, but he couldn't be sure of it because some client had turned up the volume on the jukebox to listen to a José Vélez record just at that moment.

Gregorio *el lotero*'s wife was much concerned to hear that. 'Are you sure you heard him pass up the hill?' she asked anxiously. 'Because he hasn't reached home and it's only a few hundred metres from here.'

No, the bar-owner couldn't swear to it, because he was so used to hearing Gregorio pass by each evening.

Out once more in the darkened street, Gregorio's wife tried to figure out what could have happened to her errant husband. She tried to think if there was anywhere he could have fallen somewhere between here and their house out of sight of anyone. She began to look along the row of abandoned houses in the side-street where no one had lived for at least three years since the Ayuntamiento had condemned the properties. Not bad little houses, she thought, if only they could get one of them and do it up. She couldn't think why on earth Gregorio would have left the main street and come along this deserted row. He knew this part of town all his life and wasn't likely to have got lost despite his affliction. Anyway, he had a remarkable sense of direction and could tell by the prevailing nor'-easterly breeze exactly which way he was facing. Could someone or something have attracted him off the usual route?

She approached very tentatively the ruined buildings in the street which was only faintly lit by the stars, mainly because of the fallen masonry that littered the roadway, but also because of an unreasonable fear of this forlorn spot. Suddenly she could hear a strange buzzing as of a swarm of very angry bees coming from the central buildings and then she glimpsed something light-coloured on the dark step of one of the houses. She stumbled towards the object and exclaimed loudly as she bent to pick up Gregorio's stick which was broken into pieces. Who would be so wicked as to take the stick from a blind man and leave him totally unable to find his way, she asked herself. Just then the loud buzzing noise fell to a lower note and ceased, giving way to a clatter of Morse code being transmitted. The bright bluish light of a pressure-gas lantern fell on her face as the door of the abandoned dwelling was suddenly opened and her partly uttered scream was stifled as a large, dark hand was clapped over her terrified face.

At 6.0 p.m. on 7 July, Inspector Guedes of the Miller Bajo police station in Las Palmas sat looking at his files and felt he would get nowhere in identifying the corpse found at Las Canteras Bay. His inquiries at the harbour-master's office and the shipping agents had proved fruitless: no ship had reported losing a passenger or crew-member overboard. Nor

had any of the *comisarías* on the island received any request to
trace a missing person since yesterday evening. The real
problem lay with the thousands of tourists who packed the
cheap apartment-blocks in the old capital, not to mention
those who came in at night from their hotels in the southern
resorts of Maspalomas or Playa del Inglés to whoop it up in
the discothèques and *boîtes* in Catalina Park.

But the cadaver had not borne the clothing of a tourist.
Guedes riffled through the papers in front of him until he
found the one containing the list of items found on the corpse:
a worn white shirt with its long sleeves rolled up, a grubby
grey waistcoat with a pair of two regularly spaced, arrow-
shaped perforations above the left breast-pocket, which must
have been made by a badge or some similar object. These
garments bore no makers' marks. In the left pocket of the
waistcoat there were some grains of black tobacco. The
trousers of grey sailcloth, very worn at the bottom cuffs, had
in the right side-pocket the sum of 455 pesetas in coins of
one-duro and five-duros—much more change than most
people would carry, thought Guedes. Had the victim been
some kind of itinerant vendor? The underclothes were of
an old-fashioned type, well worn and without markings,
like the trousers, which he considered very curious,
though he recalled that many of the shoddy cotton goods
sold in the Indian bazaars had no makers' tabs, as he and
his colleagues had found in other similar cases. All this
seemed to rule out a tourist or well-heeled person, though it
didn't exclude a seaman or stevedore. Did the employees
wear badges to go in and out of the naval dockyard at
Alcaravaneras? He'd better ring the duty officer there to
check.

Just then his sergeant entered with a large brown envelope. 'From the pathologist, Inspector. The report on the
unidentified corpse found at Las Canteras.'

Guedes tore open the official seal eagerly and began to
plough through the technical jargon.

The deceased was aged between 45 and 50, probably of mixed European and Guanche stock, weighing 68 kg. approx., of medium build, 1.65 m. tall, medium brown hair greying at sideboards, clean-shaven with short stubble on chin; a wound extending for 9.2 cm. from eyebrow diagonally across right temple caused by narrow rounded instrument and inflicted a few minutes before death to judge by incipient vital signs; the blow delivered with sufficient force to stun victim, causing some cerebral hæmorrhage; sea-water in nasal and buccal passages. Cause of death: asphyxial drowning in fresh water.

In fresh water? Guedes puzzled over this strange finding and read the accompanying forensic lab report on the Gettler test that had been undertaken on the sodium chlorate content of the left and right cardiac ventricles.

He was interrupted by the arrival of the old judge of instruction.

'Just thought I'd call in on my way home, Guedes, to see if you had the pathologist's report yet.'

The inspector silently handed over the file and remained silent as the ramrod-stiff judge stood reading the documents. When he had finished, he put the file down gravely.

'So what do you think, Guedes? The gash on the forehead was administered while he was still alive, as the small vital signs around the edge of the wound demonstrate, then he drowned, perhaps while unconscious from the head wound. But was it an accident? Did he stumble against the rail of a vessel thereby stunning himself and then fall into the sea, or was he struck down by an assailant and then deliberately drowned? The pathologist can't help, apparently.'

'You'd better look at these details from the lab analysis of the organs, Judge. I think they help us towards a certain conclusion, if they're accurate.'

The old judge looked hard at the young inspector and

picked up the file again, flicking the pages until he found the
path. lab report.

'Perhaps you'd care to look especially at the analysis of the
contents of the cardiac ventricles,' suggested the inspector.

The judge lit a long Canary cigar as he began to plough
through the technical language of the report, then he made a
sudden exclamation.

'Now there's a strange thing! You find him dead in shallow
sea-water and the Gettler test points to his having drowned
in fresh water. How can that be?' He looked inquiringly at
Guedes.

'I'll ask them to re-run the test, Judge, but as you see the
preliminary report definitely indicates that he was drowned
in salt-free water, and not just salt-free but filtered drinking
water.'

Then it must be a case of intentional homicide,' said the
judge gravely, 'otherwise one cannot account for this com-
bination of factors. But did it occur on shipboard or on land?
That's the problem as I see it.'

'I'll also request the lab to run further tests on the water
samples taken from the deceased,' said the inspector. 'The
amounts of chlorine, fluoride and other additives should
show whether the water is from the city's water-mains or
not.'

'Remember there are various sources of supply in the
island, Inspector. Will it help matters if we find it's from the
mains supply in the port? If the ships top up their supply of
drinking-water before sailing, isn't it likely to be the same
water as comes out of a tap on land?'

The old judge was still sharp despite his years, thought
Guedes, remembering that the judge's family owned half the
underground reservoirs in the south-western hinterland of
Gran Canaria.

'Nevertheless the lab must run tests on the type of fresh
water found in the deceased's lungs,' said the judge; 'not all
the suburbs get their supply from the same reservoir. It

depends on their relative height above sea-level. Tell them to ask the water company for samples of all the different sources that feed Las Palmas, including, of course, the supply to the port.'

'I'll do that, sir, and we'll also study the lists of missing persons, though nothing's turned up so far. I've had photographs taken of the corpse which my men will take on a house-to-house inquiry in the port area. I'm afraid that identification is going to prove difficult because of the state of the face and eyes after immersion.'

'What about the ships that entered or left the port during the past twenty-four hours?' asked the old judge. 'Have you contacted their masters?'

'The harbour-master has been in touch by radio with those that sailed and in person with those that are still in harbour. There are no reports of anyone missing.'

'I see,' sighed the judge. 'Well, carry on with your investigation, Inspector. They've managed to take fingerprints?'

'The pathologist is trying to obtain dermal prints.'

'I take it you've had the deceased's dentition examined? Anything useful there?'

'He still had most of his natural teeth, with some molars much decayed. But there's no sign of any dental work having been done. It doesn't look as though he'd ever been to a dentist except for extractions.'

'You'd better circulate copies of the dentition to the island's dentists just in case one of them recognizes it. What about the clothing? Any luck there?'

'Apart from the curious perforations in the left breast-pocket of the waistcoat, there's nothing unusual. The shirt was probably manufactured in South Korea and hundreds of them have been sold in the cheaper shops and bazaars. The trousers bore no label, but are of a very common type of heavy cotton weave. It's that pair of holes in the waistcoat pocket that intrigues me, Judge. Could they have held some kind of badge?'

'He didn't strike me as the type to be any kind of official,' commented the judge. 'Keep trying, Guedes. Perhaps you'll have some luck with the photograph.'

Consuelo Lozano found herself possessing boundless energy despite the fact that she was near to her time; in ten days or so she hoped to bear Bernal's and her first child, and the local gynæcologist, after doing a sonar scan, had hinted that it could be a girl, though she had kept this knowledge from Luis so that it should be a surprise for him. He had always said how much he wanted a daughter, after his wife Eugenia had borne him two sons—one over-pious like his mother and the other a good-time charlie like his father had once been.

Consuelo was still in the director's room at the Banco Ibérico's headquarters in the Avenida de Mesa y López in Las Palmas at 2.30 p.m. after all the senior staff had departed for lunch. She was intrigued by the curious transaction revealed by the files she was examining. Her position as personal assistant to the director, a post she held permanently in the bank's headquarters in Madrid, gave her access to virtually all the records, and her temporary boss in Gran Canaria was treating her with the entire confidence she enjoyed in Madrid; after all, the managing director himself had asked him to take her on secondment for three months as a discreet way of covering her unmarried pregnancy, about which only the local manager had been informed. None the less, she supposed the other senior staff suspected that there was more to the situation than met the eye, since her obviously advanced stage of gestation was not explained by the appearance of a 'Señor Lozano', but they were too discreet to ask questions. They had been told that she was an old and highly trusted employee of the bank and they were glad enough to make use of the expertise she had acquired in the chief office.

Consuelo Lozano had an accountant's mind and she was well used to absorbing and retaining the complex details of company accounts, in particular where there were a number of subsidiary companies with sums passing to and fro between parent and offspring. The bank had to be on the watch for signs of daisy-chain operations, in which a company with liquidity difficulties moved its small remaining credits from account to account to try and give the impression that all was well with its reserves. Here in the Las Palmas branch she had become intrigued by a local import-export business which owned bazaars in the port and tourist areas of the city where electronic goods, cameras, binoculars and typewriters were imported from the Far East and sold at apparently large discounts. But this company turned out to be just one of the numerous subsidiaries of Alcorán S.A., which had many and varied interests in the Island. Her researches had uncovered strange transfers in French francs via Paris to the subsidiaries of Alcorán S.A., which were then transferred to a holding account in the name of 'Tamarán'; what concerned her was that the debits from this last account were always made in cash to '*El Portador*—The Bearer'—and never to a named person or firm. She had only ever seen this before in cases of major defalcations and she was determined to find out more about Señor Tamarán. First she had sent a telex to the Crédit Français in Paris to try and discover the source of the large regular monthly payments into the suspect account, all of which bore the same reference number. Then she had pored over the local *listín* or telephone directory but no Señor Tamarán was listed. She called up the statements of the Alcorán account on her VDU to try to discover his address, but only that of the company offices, situated in the Ciudad Jardín area, was given.

Consuelo looked at her watch. Good Lord, was it half past four already? She hadn't felt hungry at all. Suddenly she felt a kicking inside her abdomen, and bent over in some pain until the movement ceased. She felt a thrill of joy at her imminent motherhood, and decided to call Luis before leaving the office. She dialled 91—the prefix for Madrid—and then the number of Bernal's secret apartment in the Calle de Barceló. He should be there by now, she thought. She let the number ring for a while, and then put her hand on the receiver-rest. She re-dialled for his office in the old DSE building in the Gobernación, but the duty officer told her that Superintendent Bernal had left at 1.30 and had not returned.

With a sigh, Consuelo picked up her handbag and made for the street, waving a cheery farewell to the security guard, who was the only person left in the bank's headquarters. There would be just time to call in on the registered offices of Alcorán S.A. on her way home.

Bernal watched his wife Eugenia doing the washing in the large chipped marble sink in the kitchen of their tumbledown apartment on the eighth floor of the nineteenth-century building off the Calle de Alcalá. She was vigorously rubbing bleach into his shirt-collars with a dirty-looking scrubbing-brush, and then using a bar of cheap yellow soap to rub them again on an ancient aluminium rubbing-board. He was still resentful of her refusal to use any modern assistance, such as the Zanussi automatic washing-machine he had bought her for Christmas, which stood unused, with the manufacturer's labels still intact, behind the kitchen door.

'When are you going to try out the new machine, Geñita?' he asked plaintively. 'The plumber did come and fix it in, didn't he?'

'You know how those modern contraptions rot and tear the clothes, Luis. And the plumber told me it uses a lot of electricity. I'm only sorry you had to waste all that money on a useless and unnecessary object which takes up so much room. Couldn't we ask the shop to take it back?' She glowered at the gleaming electro-domestic product. 'And there's another thing! Doña Pilar tells me that these machines magnetize the clothes and cause sparks to fly off when you iron them, which will give you cancer.'

'I'm surprised she doesn't think they'll set the house on fire as well.'

'She's more afraid of a a flood down the main staircase,' said Eugenia drily. 'She says they're always going out of control.'

Bernal declared a temporary truce at this further sign of the pigheaded and near-insane portress's bad influence on his wife, and decided to break the news of his impending departure for the Canaries.

'The Minister is sending me with my group to Las Palmas, Geñita, on a special operation. We'll be away for about a fortnight.'

'But I thought you'd be coming to Ciudad Rodrigo with me, Luis, to collect the rents from the tenants. You know I won't be able to bring back all those hams and strings of blood-sausages and barrels of olives on my own.'

'If your tenants won't pay in cash, why don't you sell all that produce locally, Geñita, and save yourself the trouble of hauling it back here? After all,' he said, gesticulating at the ceiling from which hung three fly-blown cured mountain hams and eight strings of *chorizo*, 'we never get round to eating it all, do we?'

'Are you mad, Luis? Do you know how much these hams cost here in Madrid?' She tapped the gaunt remains of one of the hams that hung from the ceiling, causing four bluebottles to fly up buzzing loudly. 'And these casks of olives that I bring back are all prepared by hand. Do you realize how long it takes to score each one and then change the brine every few days while they are soaking? The ones they sell here are really poisonous—they've just soaked them in *sosa* to take away the acid, leaving them tasting of nothing at all! If I sold them in the country I'd get next to nothing for them. Don't worry yourself! While you're living it up in Las Palmas, my brother will help me collect the half-yearly rents and then we'll put the stuff in the guard's van when we come back at the end of next month. I'll expect you for the annual village fiesta and the *encierro* and bull-run on the fifteenth of August as usual.'

'Shall I give you money to pay for the water-supply to be put in at the old *finca* there, Geñita? It seems silly to have the new bathroom and lavatory installed and then not be able to use them.'

'Such a crazy idea of yours, Luis,' she sighed. 'My parents, grandparents and great-grandparents were all content with the pump in the yard for washing and the straw in the meadow to do their business, so why should I change things?'

'But it's so unhygienic, Eugenia, and I'm tired of going round to your brother's house to shave and use the lavatory. I made it a condition for ever going there again, remember. It's a wonder there hasn't been an outbreak of typhoid or cholera in the place.'

'Stuff and nonsense, Luis. There's far more danger in the city, what with the bad *colza* or rape-seed oil that's been sold at nearly every door and poisoned those who bought it, not to mention this junk food they talk about on the television. Thank goodness for this healthy oil I pressed from our own olives. You'll be in for lunch, I take it? I'm preparing lentil and blood-sausage stew and then swordfish cutlets.'

'I'm not sure,' said Bernal, feeling strange convulsions in the scar of his gastric ulcer. 'Navarro and I have got a lot of things to organize.'

Bernal took Line 2 of the Metro from Retiro to Sol and climbed the steps into the tremendous heat of the main square, where the crowds of shoppers were assailed by the cries of gipsy women selling lottery tickets, street-vendors who set up tiny collapsible tables which they would promptly fold away at the sight of a municipal policeman, ice-cream merchants and sellers of *horchata de chufas*—that deliciously cold, milky drink made from pressed tiger-nuts which was so typical of Madrid at the height of summer. He struggled across the Calle de Carretas, now notorious for its drug-pushers, *chulos* and prostitutes of both sexes, then reached the side-door of the old Gobernación, which was shortly to be evacuated by the main Groups of the DSE. There he stopped to greet Manolo the young blind lottery-seller and chose one of the strips off the metal pad fixed to his breast-pocket.

'I hope you've taken a number ending in nine, Comisario,' the boy whispered. 'That's what I think will turn up tonight.'

'I hope you're right, Manolito. You know I've never won it in forty years.'

'Don't give up hope, Comisario! You never know when your number will come up!'

The desk-sergeant saluted the Superintendent and handed him an official envelope. 'It's about the move to the new building, Comisario. All the heads of groups have got one of these today.'

'Thank you, Emilio. I'll let Navarro handle it. Now we're coming to it, we're going to miss the old place, despite our grumbles about it over the years.'

'Have you been in the new building, Comisario? It's nothing but smoked glass and aluminium; all the rooms and corridors look the same and they're full of computers. It's like being in a space-ship.'

'If it's as bad as that, Emilio, I'm going to ask for early retirement. When are they going to move us?'

'Next week, as I've heard it on the grapevine, but that letter will probably tell you, *jefe*.'

Bernal greeted his second-in-command warmly.

'You've seen the orders about our secondment to Gran Canaria, Paco?'

'Yes, chief, and I've been in touch with all the members of the Group. Most of them will be free to leave on the midday flight tomorrow.'

'Excellent. I'd like to get away this evening, if I could. Which hotel have you booked us into?'

'I've assumed that the President's office will be paying all the expenses, chief, so I've reserved a room in the Hotel Don

Juan for you, in the Puerto de la Luz. That's the tall building shaped like a barrel that overlooks the Plaza de Santa Catalina.'

'Good. I've stayed there years ago when it was first built and it's very comfortable. Where are you staying?'

'They only had three single rooms available, so I've put the others in the Tigaday which isn't far away. I thought we'd put Elena Fernández in the Don Juan with us.'

'That's fine. We can't put her in an unsuitable place or her father will never forgive me. You'd better call them all in for a briefing at midday today so that I can explain what this security operation is all about.'

'I've already told them to come in, chief.'

'Well done. We'd better have a look at these instructions about the move to the new building, Paco. Emilio tells me it's going to be next week and we'll be away then.'

'I'd heard about it from the duty officer, chief, and I've started packing the files into boxes, but I haven't touched your desk yet.'

'I'd better get cracking then, Paco. I've got a collection of rubbish going back more than thirty years that I'll have to sort through.'

In his inner office, divided by glass panelling from the main office where there were five desks for the members of his Group, Bernal went to his chair. On the wall behind it hung a large colour photograph of the King and Queen personally signed by Their Majesties for him after a special operation he and his Group had carried out for the Palace. He decided it would be given the place of honour in his new office, assuming that there was a solid wall there on which to hang it.

He pulled open the two top drawers of his faded but solid mahogany desk and gazed unhappily at the jumble of old scraps of paper torn from notepads and an assortment of objects that had survived from past investigations. Was it worthwhile packing all this stuff into the black plastic boxes provided by the removers? He might as well throw it all away. But there might be annotations of telephone numbers, addresses and other references that could prove useful to him in future cases, if only he had the time to sort the wheat from the chaff, yet, as in all the police stations he had ever worked in, there was never any time to straighten out the paperwork. He tipped the contents of the two drawers into one of the removers' stackable boxes with a sudden flourish and then sat down to light up a Kaiser. He looked at his watch: 10.05 a.m. It would be '*una horita menos en Canarias*—one little hour less in the Canaries'—as Radio Antena 3 constantly reminded its listeners in what had become a catch-phrase. He might just contact Consuelo before she left her *chalé* for the bank if she was feeling well enough to go to work, although she was very near her time. He dialled 928-, the code for Gran Canaria, on his outside line, and looked up her number in his pocket book.

'Señora Lozano, please.' The servant-girl answered and said she would just catch the Señora before she drove away.

'Consuelo? It's Luis. I tried to get through to you yesterday evening, but the maid say you hadn't come in. Is everything OK?' He listened to the account of her shopping expedition and then broke in: 'Listen, Conchi. I've got a seat on the direct flight from Barajas to Las Palmas this evening. They've booked me into the Hotel Don Juan.'

'That's wonderful news, Luchi. I knew you'd come out if you could manage it. What's the flight number? I'll drive out to Gando airport to meet you.'

Bernal told her the flight number and the published time of arrival of the two-and-a-half-hour scheduled Iberia flight.

'Is that 9.35 p.m. local time, Luchi?'

'That's right. But I'll take a taxi if you don't feel up to driving. You must take care now. The baby's almost due, isn't it?'

'Ten days off yet, and I'm fine. I've got something interesting for you to investigate, so that you won't get bored. A holding company called Alcorán S.A. which makes very peculiar transactions. I went to see the managing director, Señor Tamarán, yesterday evening, but he was curiously unwilling to discuss his firm's accounts with me. So I've arranged another interview for this afternoon, when I'll take along copies of the strange transfers and encashments.'

'Now be careful, Consuelo; don't get involved in anything untoward, especially in your present state. The bank's got its own investigators and you won't be at that branch much longer.'

'I know that, Luchi, but when I scent something like this, you know I won't let it go.'

'I should draft you into the force. You'd be happier with us. See you tonight. By the way, the whole Group's coming out tomorrow. We're on special assignment for a fortnight.'

'I knew it! Some local investigation you've been seconded to! When will they give you a proper holiday? Still, I'm happy you'll be here with me, but I don't expect you to bring the whole Group to watch me in labour.'

'Not a chance, love.'

'*Buen viaje y muchos besos.*'

'*Igualmente.*'

The brief conversation cheered Bernal up immensely and he began to empty the remaining drawers of his desk into the black boxes with more of a will.

Soon the rest of his team came in: Inspector Juan Lista, who was so self-effacingly excellent at shadowing suspects and whose hobby was collecting bric-à-brac from the Rastro Sunday flea-market; Inspector Carlos Miranda, who was such a good investigative man in the field; and young Ángel Gallardo, the 'bad boy' of his team—a typical loose-living *madrileño*; and finally the only female member, looking as elegantly *soignée* as ever, Inspectora Elena Fernández. He went out to address them in the main office, where Paco Navarro had pinned up a large street-plan of Las Palmas and a relief map of the whole island of Gran Canaria, with its curious upturned conch-shell shape.

'Now before you rush to the conclusion that we're all going to spend our summer holidays in the Canaries at Government expense, I'd better explain what the President's office and the Minister of the Interior have asked us to do.' He noted the delighted expression on Ángel Gallardo's face. 'Another Group from the Brigada Criminal, that headed by Inspector Zurdo, who has recently been promoted to Sub-comisario, is being sent to Tenerife to perform exactly the same task as ours on Gran Canaria, and we have to keep a close liaison with him. The President of the Government will be visiting the islands for five days in the middle of this month, starting at Tenerife on the fourteenth. On the evening of the seventeenth he will fly from the new Queen Sofía airport there to Gando airport at Las Palmas in a Mystère jet provided by the Fuerza Aérea. Paco has copies of the arrangements and the routes for you to study. Our job will start the day after tomorrow, when we shall vet the security of these arrangements on the spot. We shall do this, of course, in close cooperation with the local units of the Policía Nacional, who will provide us with offices in the centre of the city.' He turned to the street-plan of Las Palmas. 'Can you point out exactly where that will be, Paco?'

Navarro took up a pointer and indicated the Gobierno Civil building in the Plaza del Ingeniero León y Castillo in the centre of the newer part of the elongated urban sprawl that constituted the capital of Gran Canaria. 'I've talked to Comisario Ramírez, the head of the local police, this morning, *jefe*, and the Civil Governor has given him instructions to offer us every facility. Unfortunately the only hotels reasonably near there, in the Parque Doramas, are fully booked. So I've booked three rooms in the Hotel Don Juan at the end of the Avenida Marítima near the Puerto de la Luz, and three others in the Hotel Tigaday nearby.'

'Can I be in the Tigaday with Elena, Paco?' asked Ángel cheekily. 'Then we can "*ripochear*" every evening.'

'What does that mean, Ángel?' inquired Elena suspiciously.

'I went there once on holiday; the Tigaday is nearly at the end of the Calle Ripoche close to Santa Catalina Square, and that's where all the action is. The locals call having a night out on the town *ripocheando* after the name of the street.'

'Elena will be in the Don Juan with Navarro and myself, Ángel, where she'll be much safer,' said Bernal firmly. 'You'd better understand at once that this is not going to be a holiday jaunt. We're going to have to peruse all the local police reports for the past month and then check them each day and night as they come in to look for any suspicious doings. You might like to take on the checking of the visitors's entry cards at the port and at Gando airport.'

Ángel groaned and tried rather unsuccessfully to look chastened. His forte in police work was to visit the clubs, discos and *boîtes* and obtain vital information about the frequenters of such haunts.

'You'll work with Juan and Carlos,' Bernal went on, 'and follow up anything suspicious. I'm flying out this evening to make contact with the local officers.'

As she left her rented villa on the Arucas road high above Las Palmas, where the air was fresher and the temperature three or four degrees cooler, Consuelo Lozano took a hasty look at the small bedroom she had fitted out as a nursery, with the pink and white butterflies and blue cornflower pattern on the wallpaper and the same motif repeated on the cot. She picked up the large transparent baby's rattle containing shiny blue glass beads which the shopkeeper had kindly presented her with when she bought the cot and layette, and slipped it into the voluminous pocket of her long flower-patterned skirt. Perhaps he wouldn't mind changing it for one with pink beads, now she knew from the specialist that the sonar scan had revealed that she was likely to give birth to a daughter. She was glad she hadn't told Luis; he had always wanted a daughter and she'd give him a pleasant surprise.

She left some last-minute instructions with the maid about the evening meal she wanted her to prepare for Luis and herself and told her she'd be in about 6.30 with the finishing touches; she'd collect Luis from the airport at 9.35 and they'd have a late *dîner intime*. She expected to have time to pick up a bottle of French champagne after her interview with the mysterious Señor Tamarán at the registered office of Alcorán S.A. at 5.0 p.m.

In the driveway of the villa, which was bordered by a splendid garden full of the spiky native variety of euphorbia, sky-blue agapanthus, maroon bougainvillea and blue and orange bird-of-paradise flowers, she got into the metallic blue Renault 5 she had hired on a three-monthly basis and slipped it into second gear as she turned on to the steep hill that was the prolongation of the Avenida de Escaleritas which led down to the newer part of the city.

Consuelo glanced at her watch: 9.25 a.m. She'd be a bit late this morning because of Bernal's call, but the traffic was always lighter after nine. She took an occasional look in the rear-view mirror and frowned suddenly as she spotted a large black Mercedes pull out from under a clump of eucalyptus trees. Hadn't she seen a similar car behind her yesterday on her way home?

When the road widened out into a dual carriageway she slowed down to 50 k.p.h. to see if the other car would pass her. Through the mirror she couldn't make out who was driving it because all its windows were of black anti-glare glass. The Mercedes at once slowed to match her speed, keeping some two hundred metres behind, and they were both passed by other impatient drivers who hooted angrily. Her interest in the Mercedes increased and she slowed further to try and read its registration number in mirror image, but apart from making out that it began with GC- for Gran Canaria the distance made it impossible to work out the rest.

When Consuelo was held up by the traffic-lights at the junction with the Paseo de Chil she looked back once more: the black Mercedes was now three cars behind her in the outer lane. She decided to make a rapid détour to see exactly what the other car was up to, and when the lights went green she turned sharply right without signalling, leaving a taxi-driver in a large white BMW cursing the folly of women drivers; Consuelo sped off southwards past the Rubio Gardens and the high monument to León y Castillo. Before the first curve in the winding Paseo de Chil she glanced back and saw no sign of the black Mercedes. At the junction with Bravo Murillo she turned quickly left towards the Las Palmas quay at San Roque and then north again on the Avenida Marítima that would lead her back to Las Alcaravaneras beach and the bank in Mesa y López. She parked the Renault in the shade of a large catalpa tree and easing her considerable bulk out of the driving-seat looked up and down the street; there was no sign of her pursuers. As she entered the cool portals of the Banco Ibérico she glanced back through the smoked-glass doors: the black Mercedes was just pulling up on the other side of the street.

Inspector Guedes sat in his office in the Miller Bajo police-station looking through the night reports and the previous day's list of missing persons from all the *comisarías* on the island of Gran Canaria. These had been consolidated and re-circulated to all the stations. His, as usual, led the field for the number of incidents, with Playa del Inglés and Maspalomas close runners-up. These were the areas where foreign and national tourists were concentrated and most of the reports concerned street-muggings, lost property, car thefts, burglary, drug-pushing, public-scandal offences and two cases of attempted rape. There were only three reports of missing persons: a male German tourist aged 53 reported missing by his anxious wife at Playa del Inglés, a twelve-year-old girl at Arucas, and a seventy-nine-year-old man at

Mogan in the south-west of the island. Guedes read the
description of the missing German with care: very stout
(weight 105 kg. approx.), 1.85 m. tall, bald apart from a
close-cropped blond-white ring of hair at the sides, small
moustache of same colouring; a reproduction of his passport
photo would be sent to all stations shortly. The German had
disappeared on 6 July, the same night as the unidentified
man found at Las Canteras had died, but there was clearly
no physical resemblance.

Guedes read through the remaining reports more quickly,
and his eye was caught by one other item: a middle-aged
woman, without documentation to identify her, had been
found unconscious at 6.30 a.m. that morning at the corner of
the Calle del Faro and Coronel Rocha at the top of La Isleta.
She was badly concussed by a savage blow administered to
her left temple and still had not recovered consciousness.
She was in critical condition in the UVI or intensive care
unit of the Clínica Santa Catalina. The prognosis was
grave.

Guedes's interest was caught by the similarity of the injury
to that suffered by the unknown cadaver found at Las
Canteras Bay. He went over to the street-plan on the wall:
the spot where she had been found, actually an hour or so
before he had been called to the discovery of the man's
corpse, was some three hundred metres immediately above
the rocks where the drowning victim had lain. Could there be
a connection? Perhaps the old judge was wrong in supposing
the man's body had fallen off a ship.

Guedes decided to send one of his men to the clinic to stand
by in case the woman recovered consciousness. In the meantime he sent for the national policemen who had submitted
the report on finding the woman. The patrol car was called
in by radio and the two beige-and-brown-uniformed men
entered Guedes's office, holding their folded brown berets in
their right hands.

After they had saluted him, Guedes asked: 'How did you

come upon this unconscious woman in Coronel Rocha? Did you receive a call?'

'No, sir,' answered the older of the two men. 'We were on our first patrol of the day in the Isleta district. We drove up the Calle del Faro and as we turned into Coronel Rocha I spotted a shape among the litter and fallen masonry in front of a row of deserted houses.'

'Show me exactly where on the map.'

The policeman approached the street-plan and pointed to the spot. 'Just here, sir. Near the volcanic rocks that lead up to the radio-station of the coastguards.'

'What was she wearing?'

'A dirty grey and white polka-dotted dress and blue rope-soled sandals. She had no purse and no means of identification on her. We radioed for an ambulance when we found she had a weak pulse still and was breathing shallow. She had a nasty gash on the left temple, as though she had been mugged.'

'Did you question any of the people living nearby?'

The two policemen looked aggrieved. 'There aren't any, sir,' said the younger man. 'All those dwellings were abandoned more than a year ago.'

'And did you look into any of the empty buildings? There may have been dossers or drop-outs hanging out there.'

'There was no one, sir,' the men replied stolidly.

'What impression did you form at the scene? Did it look as though she had been attacked for her purse, or as though she had stumbled in the dark and hit her head?'

'Difficult to tell, sir,' said the older policeman. 'The gash on her head could have been caused by the pavement edge if she had fallen.'

'But what was she doing there in the first place, eh?' asked Guedes. 'I think I'd better go up there and take a look. Are you men still on duty?'

'Yes, sir, for another hour yet. We've been working the split shift today.'

'Good. You can drive me up there and show me exactly how she was lying when you found her. Is there anything else either of you can recall?'

'Only the sliver of light-coloured wood, sir. She was clutching it tightly in her right hand. Neither we nor the ambulance-men could get her to leave go of it.'

'She didn't speak at all?'

'Not a word, sir. She groaned a bit when we lifted her on to the stretcher, but then lapsed into unconsciousness.'

At 2.30 p.m. Consuelo Lozano gathered up her notes on the accounts of Alcorán S.A. and went out to the photocopying machine in the main office to take copies of the suspect transfer-slips, bearer-cheques and bank statements, in order to discuss the whole matter with the mysterious Señor Tamarán, who had declined to receive her the previous day. Then she perused once more the telex message she had received from the Crédit Français in Paris which informed her that the regular monthly credits of 150,000 francs to the account of Alcorán S.A. originated in their branch in Algiers. Only a reference number was given on the paying-in slips.

Consuelo decided not to show the telex to Señor Tamarán, and tucked it in the drawer of her desk. But she would ask him about the large monthly payments in pesetas to Bearer, which didn't appear to correspond to any transaction of his companies. She wondered if Alcorán S.A. had properly audited balance-sheets deposited with the Registro de Sociedades and made annual returns to Hacienda. She didn't think it proper to ask the tax authorities about a client's affairs, but she could seek a copy of the most recent balance-sheet from the Registrar of Companies. She could then calculate how much Alcorán and its subsidiaries were indebted to the Banco Ibérico at any particular stage of what appeared to be an illicit daisy-chain of credits undertaken to maintain an artificial appearance of liquidity in each company's account.

On her way to the lift, Consuelo waved goodbye to the director of the branch. She hesitated a moment, wondering whether she ought not tell him about her worries over the Alcorán accounts. No, she'd better wait until she had definite proof. As she emerged from the lift in the marble-floored and walled vestibule, she suddenly remembered the black Mercedes. Perhaps she should mention it to the director or to the head of bank security, but she had no access to the keys of the vaults, so she'd be useless to any prospective bank-robbers. Of course they wouldn't know that, and she'd read about managers and their families being held hostage until the strong-rooms were opened for the thieves. Perhaps she'd better take a peep and point the car out to the security guard if it was there.

She looked carefully up and down the street through the anti-glare glass of the front doors, but couldn't see the suspicious vehicle. Consuelo shrugged and emerged on to the street. Perhaps her imagination was playing tricks on her; after all, she hadn't been able to read the *matrícula* of the black limousine and therefore couldn't be sure that it was the same car that she had seen on each occasion.

Shaking off her fears, she made her way to the Renault and eased herself into the driving seat, suddenly remembering the blue rattle in the right-hand pocket of her wide skirt as it shook against the door-handle. She couldn't go and change it for a pink one now; the shop would have closed at 1.30. She suddenly felt the child stir within her; it wouldn't be long now. She had a sudden craving for shellfish, so decided to drive south along the coastal highway until she could find a restaurant specializing in them with a pleasant terrace overlooking the sea. Perhaps she'd find one at San Cristóbal; there was plenty of time before her appointment with the hitherto faceless Señor Tamarán.

Inspector Guedes was driven in the white SEAT patrol car out of the narrow Calle Tomás Miller, where his *comisaría* was, into Alfredo Jones and thence to Albareda which led from Las Palmas proper to La Isleta. The driver turned left at the old theatre and sped along Ferrer and from there on to the steep Calle del Faro. At the summit Guedes could see the military radio station perched on the upper slopes of the bleak volcanic clinker and beyond it the old Nissen huts that had served as a concentration camp for Republican prisoners during and after the Civil War.

They parked the patrol car at the corner of Coronel Rocha.

'That's where we found her, sir,' said the older policeman, pointing to the row of deserted one-storey houses, 'lying half in the gutter with her left hand stretched out towards that doorway.'

Guedes inspected the débris on the ground carefully and bent to pick up a long sliver of polished, light-coloured wood, which he placed in a plastic bag. 'Was this the kind of wood she was clutching?'

The patrolman looked at it. 'Could be, sir.'

'It seems to be part of a larger object, perhaps a baton or cane. See if either of you can spot the rest of it.'

Guedes crouched to inspect a number of large-tread tyre-marks in the dusty roadway, which were partly softened by the keen breeze. He approached the doorway of the nearest of the dwellings, the doors and windows of which were boarded up.

'Someone's loosened the boarding over this door. Did you look inside?'

'Nothing in there, sir.'

'I'll take a look anyway. Have you got a torch?'

'I'll get one from the car, sir.'

Guedes examined first the doorstep, and then the boarding, which showed signs of having been forced open with a crowbar. Then he shone the powerful beam of the torch over the large outer room of the abandoned house. The only furniture consisted of an old plank-top table and two broken chairs with raffia seats. He spotted a pool of dark liquid in the far corner of the room, and gently dipped his forefinger in it to sniff at it. Diesel oil for sure. Under the table he caught sight of some clippings of white electrical flex with the red, blue and brown insulation showing at each end. Rather strange, he thought, since there had never been any electricity installed in these dwellings.

He noticed a faint odour of kerosene as he moved cautiously past the tumbledown door that led to the smaller back room, which was completely unfurnished apart from an abandoned ten-litre petrol-can which he shook gently. It was empty. The back door was ajar and it creaked as he pulled it wider and looked out at the rising mass of volcanic rocks. Just outside the door he was surprised to see a large oil-drum half full of dirty water. Yet there was no supply of running water nearby and it hadn't rained for many months past. Also in the rear yard were some broken pieces of white matchwood which looked as though they had formed part of a large cigar-box. These too Guedes placed in a plastic bag for later forensic examination. When he was about to return to the street he noticed on the basalt doorstep some dark star-shaped stains each with a comet-like tail facing the oil-drum. Almost certainly blood-stains, he concluded.

Guedes emerged once more into the débris-covered street.

'I want to use your car radio to get the forensic chaps up here,' he told the two patrolmen. 'I want you to stand guard until I can send for reliefs. Then you can go off duty.'

The inspector called in to give instructions and then strolled across to the edge of the rocks overlooking Confital Bay. The north-east trades blew strongly across El Morro de la Vieja—'The Snout of the Old Woman'—as the highest peak of La Isleta was called, and down on to the volcanic slope where Guedes stood. He shivered and wondered what had occurred in this lonely spot during the long hours of the night. He was joined by the two patrolmen and they looked down at the clinker rocks below which were littered with an incredible assortment of refuse: old clothes, broken furniture,

rusted tin cans and squashed cardboard boxes as far as the
eye could see.

'It's a nightmare,' commented Guedes. 'It would take
months to sort out this lot.'

Consuelo Lozano enjoyed her lunch which had consisted of a
platter of locally caught seafood and now sat drinking coffee
on the terrace of the modest restaurant overlooking the castle
of San Cristóbal and the waves breaking on the rocks
beyond. It was cloudy as usual in the north of the island, but
a warm breeze blew across her face. She opened her briefcase
and took another look at the Alcorán papers and after a while
started making notes of the specific questions she would put
to Señor Tamarán.

At 4.30 she decided she'd better drive back into the city
centre in order to allow time to find a parking place. She
drove carefully along León y Castillo and reached the Parque
Doramas without seeing any sign of the ominous black
Mercedes. She turned into the street where the Alcorán
offices were and looked for a parking space. As she'd expected, there was no room at all, so she began to try the
side-streets. Finally she found a small gap and spent some
time manœuvring into it, employing the usual national
method of bumping sharply into the car parked at either end
of hers at each tack. After locking the car she began to walk
towards the main street when she was shaken to see a black
Mercedes with anti-glare windows parked at the corner. It
looked identical to the one that had followed her and she
stopped to take a note of the registration number. Then she
made off boldly for the interview with Señor Tamarán.

Superintendent Luis Bernal had packed his suitcase while
Eugenia was at early morning Mass, and he'd called in for
his usual breakfast of toasted croissant and coffee at Félix
Pérez's bar before setting off for the Gobernación to give
Paco Navarro last-minute instructions about the Las Palmas

operation. They had agreed that he should make contact with Comisario Ramírez as soon as he arrived in order to ensure that there would be a proper liaison with the local force, which they had no wish to antagonize.

Bernal had one errand to perform before lunch. He walked across the completely unshaded Puerta del Sol in the intense July heat and was glad to reach the shadowy side of Montera, a sloping street full of shoe-shops and prostitutes which led to the Red de San Luis and the Gran Vía. There in the stuffy heat-haze he made for the Casa del Libro, the largest and best-stocked bookshop in Madrid—probably in the whole country—where he lingered longest on the first floor in the section comprising the economic and political history of the Canaries. Always thorough, when a case took him outside his normal habitat of Madrid, which he knew from top to toe, he liked to do a little preparatory research. Armed with three recent publications, he made for the cash-desk: at least he'd have something to read on the plane or during the usually inevitable delays at Barajas airport.

On the way back to Sol, he went via the Calle de Tres Cruces and stopped at José's bar opposite the new Príncipe theatre. The excursion had left him perspiring and breathless and José, knowing his old client, served him a *doble* of draught beer without asking him first.

At 5.30 p.m. Bernal said goodbye to Eugenia, who was in the oratory cupboard off the living-room cleaning the excess candle-wax from the holders in front of the half-life-size image of Our Lady of the Sorrows before which she frequently made prayers.

'I shall expect to see you on the tenth of August for the start of the village fiesta, Luis,' she said firmly. 'Don't let me down this year.'

'Only on condition you get the local plumber to connect up the water-supply to the house. Is it a deal?'

Eugenia grunted noncommittally, and turned back to her task.

At 5.35 p.m. Bernal took a taxi to Barajas, where he was surprised to see so few passengers in the Terminal Nacional. He checked in at an Iberia desk for the direct Boeing 737 flight to Las Palmas and decided to have a coffee and a Carlos III *coñac* in the departure lounge. On seeing the amount the barman wrote on the chit, he was glad the President's office was paying all his expenses.

When he finally boarded the half-empty Club section of the plane, the air-hostess offered him a selection of newspapers. He chose the two published in the Canaries and began to leaf through them. Suddenly he sat up with a jerk. One of the news-sheets had published full details of the President's forthcoming visit to Tenerife and Gran Canaria, including the detailed dates and timings, and two route-plans. Bernal was appalled at this sign of lax security, and determined to have words with the Civil Governor as soon as he arrived.

Consuelo Lozano took the lift to the fourth floor and entered the small but elegant offices of Alcorán S.A. where she found no one, since she had arrived somewhat early. The door of one of the private offices was ajar and she glimpsed a tall, blond, middle-aged man with his head turned towards the window, who was speaking in a soft Canaries accent to a girl who wasn't in Consuelo's line of vision.

'When she arrives, put her in Ramón's office and ask her for the papers, will you?'

'But she was insistent that she must see Señor Tamarán personally. What shall I tell her?'

The man turned his head and caught sight of Consuelo. He made a gesture and the door was suddenly closed.

Consuelo sat down in the open-plan outer office and wondered if this was the man she needed to see. A few minutes passed and nobody emerged. It struck Consuelo that there was really very little business activity in these offices, which were smaller than she had expected. She began to prowl about the vestibule and took a look at what the secretary had been typing: it was clearly the start of a business letter addressed to a Señor Mencey in the Rue Lafayette, Algiers.

Seeing little else of interest, she started to walk along the corridor, looking idly at the reproductions of early prints of *La muy noble y leal Ciudad de Las Palmas* which adorned the walls, and stopped at a half-open door behind which she could hear a loud humming noise, produced, she thought, by an electric fan or extractor. She looked up and down the corridor and, seeing no one, decided to risk peeping into the room.

The office was large and lit only artificially by neon tubes. It contained a teletype machine, which accounted for the electronic hum, and beyond it what she judged to be a large and sophisticated radio transmitter and receiver. But what attracted her interest most were two large wall-plans of the north-eastern part of Gran Canaria and the city of Las Palmas itself, which bore coloured ribbons indicating routes. At a number of points black discs containing numbers or figures had been placed over the ribbons, and underneath the plan was a legend in large type: MENCEY PLAN. Mencey? Wasn't the letter in the typewriter addressed to a man of that name in Algiers? She was afraid to enter the radio-room to take a closer look, and just then heard a door opening.

The dyed-blonde secretary looked suspiciously at her as she emerged from the inner corridor.

'I'm Consuelo Lozano and I've an appointment with Señor Tamarán. I was just looking for a lavatory. It's pressure on the bladder, you know,' she whispered confidentially. 'I'm near my time.'

'Anyone could see that,' said the haughty secretary laconically. 'It's the second door on the right.'

When Consuelo emerged from a brief visit to the facilities, which she had employed to repair her make-up, she noted that the door to the radio-room was now firmly shut.

Señor Tamarán, if it was he, received her with the shy and softly complacent manner typical of his race, and ushered her to a chair.

'Are you feeling all right, Señora? Is there anything we can get you?'

'I'm fine, thanks. I wanted a private word with you, Señor Tamarán, before taking things any further with my superiors at the Bank,' Consuelo began, opening her black hide brief-case to take out the photocopies of the Alcorán statements. 'I would be grateful for your comments on some of these transfers.'

'May I see the papers, Señora?' The fair-haired man with the yellowish complexion stood up and came to her side.

'I've marked in red ink the chain of debits and credits from one subsidiary to another as I see them,' commented Consuelo. 'As you will note, these range over a period of more than eight months.'

He took the papers from her and went back to sit at his desk. 'I'm afraid I can't be of much use to you, Señora. Our chief accountant has gone on holiday and only he really understands the financial side of things.'

Consuelo gulped at this. 'But you are listed as *Administrador único*,' she pointed out. 'Don't you keep watch over the balance-sheets of your companies?'

'Of course, but he's always here to explain them to me. He'll be back on the first of August.'

'And what happens if there's a financial crisis before then?' asked Consuelo sweetly.

'Oh, we'd weather it, I suppose,' he answered vaguely. 'There's less business from July to September.'

'But I thought you imported and exported tourist goods, Señor Tamarán. Wouldn't there be the summer trade to supply?'

'Our high season is from December to April, Señora. The

retailers will be stocking up again in the autumn.' He handed the photocopies back to her.

Consuelo thought she'd better turn to the matter of the cheques drawn to bearer. 'Perhaps you'd care to look at these payments out of the main Alcorán account. Can you explain them?'

The man's face darkened with sudden rage. 'What business is that of the Bank?' he demanded. 'These payments are a matter for the company.'

'But you must admit that they are unusual,' she persisted. 'They are made out for the same large amount every month. Perhaps they are the rent for some premises, or the salary of someone who insists on being paid in cash? Either way, they are very large sums, and would no doubt be accounted for in your annual balance-sheet.'

'Señora, in the event of having to give explanations, we shall provide them to the Registrar of Companies and to Hacienda, but not to you,' he concluded coldly.

'I estimate that your companies have a debit to us of more than five million pesetas, taken on average across a normal month's working,' Consuelo persisted in a deadly tone. 'This debit is disguised by the recycling of the same liquid sum. I think you'd better get your chief accountant back from his holiday, because if you can't give me a satisfactory explanation by tomorrow morning, I shall have no option but to pass the matter to the Bank's senior investigator in Madrid.'

On this note Consuelo considered it wise to storm out, leaving Tamarán speechless with fury. She almost fell over the ash-blonde secretary who had obviously been listening at the keyhole.

Once in the street, Consuelo calmed down and decided to look for a *bodega*; she might as well buy the champagne and the other things she needed for the special reunion dinner with Luis. Then she could go home for a rest before setting out to meet him at the airport.

*

At 8.0 p.m. on the same evening, Inspector Guedes was called to the Santa Catalina clinic by his *cabo* or corporal, who told him the doctors believed that the unknown woman found in the Calle del Coronel Rocha might briefly recover consciousness, although the prognosis remained critical.

At the clinic which overlooked Las Alcaravaneras beach Guedes found his man sitting outside the glass door of the intensive care unit.

'She's groaned once or twice, Inspector, but they say she's still deeply comatose. They've noticed occasional activity on the encephalograph machine. There's a nurse talking to her all the time to try and bring her out of it.'

Guedes asked to speak to the doctor in charge. 'Can you get her out of the coma sufficiently to ask who she is, Doctor?' he asked.

'There's nothing we can do that we aren't already doing, Inspector. She's on a life-support machine. The cerebral scan indicates massive damage and there's no hope of recovery in my opinion.'

Just then the nurse emerged to call the doctor back. 'She's trying to say something, I think.'

'Can I go in?' asked Guedes.

'There's no harm in it,' said the doctor. 'Keep talking to her softly and reassuringly and she may respond.'

Guedes noted that the injured woman was in her fifties, with greying hair, and she had a large sticking-plaster over the gash on her left temple. Her left eye was blackened and closed, while her right eyelid fluttered a little.

'Can you tell me your name, Señora?' he began in a quiet, kindly tone. 'We want to help you. You are in good hands here. Are you comfortable?'

After a while the lips began to form words, and Guedes watched to see if he could make them out. 'Could you moisten her lips and tongue?' he asked the nurse, who gently dabbed at the patient's mouth with cottonwool soaked in a mild boracic solution.

The woman suddenly clenched her right hand and her lips moved. 'My hus . . . band . . . Where's . . . my . . . hus . . . band . . .' The attempt to speak failed.

'What's your name, Señora?' urged Guedes. 'Tell us your name and we'll be able to find your husband. Please give us your name and address.'

Again the eyelid fluttered and the lips began to shape sounds. 'Ro . . . sa . . . rio.'

'Yes, yes,' said Guedes eagerly. 'Rosario. Do tell us: what else?'

Once more there was an articulatory effort. 'Par . . . di . . . lla.'

'Pardilla? Rosario Pardilla? Is that your name?'

The woman's head turned twice in a jerking movement towards the pillow, and she spoke no more. The doctor checked the monitoring instruments. 'I'm afraid she's relapsed into deep coma. There's very little brain activity now.'

'Do you think she said "Rosario Pardilla"?' Guedes asked the nurse.

'That's right, Inspector.'

'Could I see the clothing she was wearing when she was admitted? It might provide more clues.'

'I doubt it,' replied the nurse. 'We checked it carefully and there's nothing to help in identifying her. But I'll get it for you.'

'I'll take it to Forensic just in case. We'll check the electoral lists for Rosario Pardilla, and get in touch with Documento Nacional de Identidad. It's a pity she hasn't given us her second surname, but perhaps there won't be many Pardillas on the island.' Guedes turned to the doctor. 'I'll leave a man here, if you don't mind, to inform me at once if she comes round again.'

'It's most unlikely, Inspector. Her pulse-rate is failing and there's nothing more we can do.'

*

After laying the table for two and placing pale pink candles in a pair of silver-plated three-branched candelabra, Consuelo Lozano surveyed the scene. Yes, it was sufficiently homely yet romantic at the same time, or it would be by 10.0 p.m. with the moonlight and the heavy scent of the jasmine from the porch outside. She told the maid when to start cooking the chicken fricassée, which would best suit Luis's delicate stomach, and she made sure the avocados stuffed with prawns were chilling in the refrigerator.

'I'm leaving now, Manolita. If the plane's on time, we should be here by ten or soon after.'

'I'm so pleased for you, Señora, that your husband will be with you for the confinement.'

'I'll be surprised if he is,' commented Consuelo drily. 'Detectives always get up to something.'

As she swung the Renault out on to the main road and switched on the dipped headlights in the gathering dark, she had put the black Mercedes entirely out of her mind, so that she didn't notice when it slipped out of the clump of eucalyptus trees and followed her down the hill at a discreet distance.

When Consuelo turned right at the Paseo de Chil and then south at the end of it on to the main highway, she concentrated on the thick traffic with only one part of her mind while pondering how she would now arrange her future life with an illegitimate child—illegitimate for certain, because Luis wouldn't be able to obtain a divorce from Eugenia against her will for at least two years even under the new legislation.

Consuelo had informed her brother and sister-in-law, of course, since they were at present looking after their widowed mother, but now she would be faced with breaking the news. Her mother would certainly affect to be horrified at the social stigma she would see in it, but perhaps little by little she would take to her grand-daughter and gain a new interest in life. She had sunk into the penumbra of widowhood too easily after her husband's death from liver cancer nine years ago, and had too much time on her hands.

Soon Consuelo saw the sign for Gando and took the next exit. Now she could see the airport lights and she made for the car-park in front of the terminal building. As she switched off the engine and began to get out, a dark metallic shape slewed to a halt across the bows of the Renault and two men jumped out. Oh God, it was the black Mercedes which she had forgotten all about. She tried to slam the door shut and put the lock-button down, hoping to start the car and reverse out of the space across the concrete ramp under the canopy of dried palm-fronds, but the men forced the door open and the first of them stuck a pistol into her side.

'Move over, lady, we're going for a little ride.'

'But I can't!' she yelled, hoping someone would hear her. 'I'm pregnant, can't you see.'

He clamped his left hand over her mouth and she bit it fiercely. He gave a yelp and snatched his hand back quickly.

'Lady, this thing's loaded. Believe it.'

In the meantime the second man advanced upon her with a large piece of sticking-plaster and clamped it over her mouth, while the first man twisted her right arm behind her, forcing her against the steering-wheel.

'Now move over, lady. We'll not tell you again.'

Gradually she managed to squeeze herself across the hand-brake, but she felt something crush as she passed the gear-lever. She landed untidily on the front passenger seat while the first man snatched the keys from her hand and the second got into the rear, bringing her arms to the back of the seat and tying her wrists together.

The driver of the black Mercedes now pulled away and the first of her abductors started up the Renault and began to follow it. Realizing that there was no immediate hope of escape, she tried to calm herself, breathing rhythmically through her nostrils. She tried to steal a glance at the driver of her car. He wasn't Spanish, she had thought from his accent, and now she could see that he was rather dark-complexioned, with a Semitic profile. Could he be an Arab or Berber? she wondered. She concentrated on the direction the cars were taking, for at least they hadn't blindfolded her. She saw they were leaving Gando on the old minor road that led to Telde—the second town of Gran Canaria—which tourists rarely visited. She had only been there once to visit a manufactory of local crafts.

When the rapidly moving car shook her from side to side as the driver savagely cut the curves on the rough and narrow road, Consuelo again felt something crack at her right side. Then she remembered the transparent baby's rattle with the blue beads in the deep pocket of her skirt; she wouldn't be able to change it for one with pink beads now! Then she had an idea of how it might turn out to be useful to her, if only they would release her hands.

She watched the road-signs carefully as they turned north at a wider road, then she saw lights as they approached some houses. And there was the sign: TELDE. The car slowed as they entered the almost deserted town—everyone must be dining, she thought—and soon the driver of her Renault flashed his headlights at the Mercedes, enabling her to see its registration number for the first time. It was the same as the one she had noted down near the offices of Alcorán S.A. So this was no ordinary criminal abduction to hold her for a ransom or for the keys to the bank vault; the enigmatic Señor Tamarán must have ordered it.

The driver of the Mercedes switched his rear lights on and off twice and then sped off towards Las Palmas. The Renault was now turned off the main street and Consuelo got confused as they entered a maze of narrow side-streets consisting of whitewashed single-storey houses. The car pulled up outside a dwelling on the edge of town. To the east of Telde, Consuelo told herself; they hadn't re-crossed the main road that ran north-south through the town.

The driver switched off the lights and got out. He knocked

at the door of the hovel, which was opened by a teenage girl who looked frightened. The abductor in the back seat spoke to Consuelo in a soft but menacing voice:

'If you behave, lady, and do exactly as I tell you, no harm will come to you. Now I'm going to release your arms and then we'll take the gag off you. If you scream or try to attract attention, I'll kill that child you're bearing.' He pushed the pistol into her swollen belly. 'Do you understand?'

Consuelo nodded vigorously. The driver now returned carrying a bunch of keys.

'Here we go, then, lady, and no tricks now.'

Again Consuelo noted the foreign accent and the slurred pronunciation. When they had untied her hands and removed the sticking-plaster, she rubbed her wrists slowly and whispered to the man who was getting out of the rear seat and who she guessed was the pleasanter of the pair, 'Can I have a drink of water?'

'I'll give you something to drink,' said the driver, handing her a hip-flask.

Consuelo wondered if she should try to sound the horn and cry out. But seeing the deserted street and the dark spread of sandy waste in front of her, she decided it would be useless, and even counter-productive.

'Now come out slowly,' said the driver, waving his pistol at her.

As she moved her stiff limbs, Consuelo slipped her hand into the pocket of her skirt and grasped hold of the rattle, which had broken in two along its join. She caught hold of a clutch of the beads that had fallen out of it, half the frame of the rattle and a silk handkerchief. 'Can I take out a hankie?' she asked.

'Go ahead, but slowly does it now.'

She tried to wrap the handkerchief round the rattle, retaining a number of the beads in the palm of her hand. Then she slowly removed her hand and brought the handkerchief to her nose.

'Get out slowly now.'

Taking advantage of the gloom, she let the plastic frame fall from her hand to the gutter and put her foot on it as she stood up. 'Can I have that drink of water?'

'Here you are; it'll do you good.'

She took a deep draught from the hip-flask and gasped as she realized it was cheap brandy or *aguardiente*.

'That'll put some spirit into you!' said the man, chuckling. 'Now come with us.'

They led her towards the dark countryside beyond the last of the houses, and she took the opportunity of letting a few beads fall from her hand on to the pavement and into the hollow of a storm-drain. The street itself was lit only by occasional pools of light emanating from old-fashioned lamps with white glass half-shades mounted on the roofs of the houses; but on the wasteland there was only the light of the moon, rising full and red-coloured over the African Sea. Was this the end? she asked herself. Were they meaning to do away with her here in this lonely spot?

Then she saw the bulk of a large open farm truck with a tattered canvas roof.

'If you behave yourself, we'll just tie your left arm to the seat and leave you with one arm free,' said the second abductor. 'I'll be alongside you with this,' and he waved the pistol at her.

She got in slowly, without being prompted, and they ordered her to sit in the second row of wooden slatted seats. It was going to be a rough ride, she anticipated. The child stirred within her and she bent forward and groaned quietly. She took the chance of dropping more beads on to the floor of the truck or farm wagon, which she was delighted to see had rough wooden planks loosely nailed together on the floor and its back open to the wind. With luck some of the beads would roll off on to the roadway if she dropped some every so often. Consuelo could think of no other way of leaving any kind of trail behind her.

The second abductor now bound her arm to the wooden support of the bench-like seat and then went round to sit beside her. The driver had difficulty in starting the engine of the rickety vehicle, which smelled strongly of bananas.

'Now I'm going to blindfold you,' said her guard. 'It's better for you not to know where we're going.'

She began to protest as he took out a bandana and tied it roughly across her eyes, making a knot behind her head.

'Where's my handbag?' she asked with sudden concern.

'Don't worry, we've got it safe.' She bet they had searched it already.

The truck lumbered over the wasteland behind the houses, and Consuelo found she could see a little by squinting down her nose, but she refrained from lifting her head in order not to reveal this to her captors. She noted that they had reached a smoother surface and could glimpse some light from a street-lamp. She tried to remember the turns they took, but soon got hopelessly confused. Surely they would return to the main road that ran through Telde, so she should watch out for the driver to halt before turning into the main street, and then she must observe whether he turned left or right.

After a while, the truck slowed and then stopped briefly. The little light she could see from under the scarf seemed much brighter. This must be the main highway running through the town. Should she risk shouting for help? But the engine was very noisy and the street might be deserted at this hour. Dear God, she thought suddenly, it must be ten o'clock or so. Luis would have landed and been looking for her at the airport! What would he do when he didn't find her there? Surely he would ring up the villa. The maid would tell him that her mistress had set out at nine o'clock and he would assume that she had had a puncture or a breakdown, or even an accident. What would he do then? But now she must concentrate on where her abductors were taking her.

The wagon was turning left, southward to Maspalomas, then. She let three more beads drop on to the floor, hoping they would swing out onto the asphalt. How many did she have left in the palm of her hand? It felt like a dozen or so. When they were all gone she would make an excuse to put her hand back into her pocket to try and reach the remainder.

Now she could hear vehicles passing them in the opposite direction and occasionally they themselves were overtaken by a fast-moving car or a *guagua*—one of the rickety local buses. She must pay attention to any deviation they made from the southern highway. When she could still glimpse some light from the street-lamps of Telde, the truck lurched to the right on to a rougher surface and the driver changed down to third. Consuelo quickly dropped the beads that remained in her hand. Now there was no light at all as the engine took on a whining note on the steep upward incline. She was shaken from side to side by the curving road. They must have turned off the main highway, she reasoned; the road to the south was smoother and less hilly than this. They were taking her up into the mountains of the interior, but were they on the road to San Mateo?

She had been taken along that road once when the bank manager and his wife had invited her out to lunch at the Parador de Tejeda, when they had stopped at Teror to see the wooden image of Nuestra Señora del Pino, the patron saint of Gran Canaria. If so, there should be occasional traffic passing them, but so far she had heard none. She lifted her head gently to see if she could see anything through the gap under the blindfold, but all was in near-darkness apart from a pale reflection from the moonlit landscape and a faint yellow glow from the dashboard. The air was getting much cooler as they climbed, and Consuelo began to shiver.

The captor alongside her was having difficulty in lighting a cigarette; she could see the flare of his lighter as he cupped his hands against the strong breeze. She took the chance of plunging her right hand which held the handkerchief into the deep pocket of her skirt and wrapped it round the remaining piece of the broken rattle. She also grabbed a few of the remaining beads. Had her captor noticed? She held her breath. Very slowly she extracted her hand.

'Is it much further?' she asked, in order to distract him.

'Not much. Then you'll get something to eat.'

'Why are you doing this to me? It must be a mistake. I'm not rich or important, you can be sure of that.'

'Keep her trap shut,' yelled the driver, swearing as he struggled with the heavy gear lever on the mountain road.

Afraid they would gag her once more, Consuelo kept silent. Then she raised her head slowly and glimpsed a white roadsign some distance ahead which was reflected in the high beam of the truck's headlights. She had a brief glimpse of the name as it flashed by: VALLE something; there were two more words that she hadn't been able to read. The truck slowed as they wound through the village street, and she moved her right arm across as though to ease the bond on her left wrist. She was watching for the sign marking the end of the village which would have a red diagonal bar across the place-name. She screwed up her eyes; yes, there it was: VALLE LOS NUEVES.

The name meant nothing to her, but as the truck began to gain more speed, she quietly dropped the remains of the rattle over the side into the roadway. She held her breath again: her captors hadn't noticed, apparently. She squeezed her right palm to see what else she had: only five or six beads now. She'd have to space them out. If only she knew how far they were going.

Now it got really cold and she realized they must have climbed way above the height where her villa stood at about 300 metres above sea-level at Las Palmas. Were they taking her towards Pozo de las Nieves, which was one of the highest cones on the island after the Roque Nublo? There was no light at all now apart from the faint and ghostly glow of the moonlit landscape. Then they began to descend on a steep twisting track, and the driver had to change down to second.

She guessed that they were entering one of the volcanic *calderas*. Not all these large craters left by ancient eruptions could be entered by wheeled vehicles, and she had read that the aborigines had made their last stand against the Spaniards in one of them. Was it Tirajana? She couldn't remember now. The Republican *maquis* during the Civil War had made use of them and famous bandits had hidden out in them in modern times too; very recently a kidnapped industrialist had been hidden away in one of them for more than three months. Was this the same gang?

'It won't be long now,' muttered the captor at her side, who more and more gave the impression of being less ruthless than the driver. This cued her to drop the remaining beads in one go, and she drew the handkerchief to her mouth to dissimulate her action.

The truck lurched to a stop and the more friendly of her captors unbound her eyes.

'You'll be given some supper now.'

He untied her left arm and prodded her gently to alight. It was very dark and she opened and shut her eyes a few times to be sure she was seeing properly. The sky was lit by the moon but little light penetrated into this valley. She had the feeling that there was a towering mass of rock above where the truck now stood with its radiator emitting ghostly clouds of steam. More men appeared carrying hurricane lamps and they began to confer in low voices with the driver. The other man led her towards the rocks where he pushed open a wooden door and indicated she was to enter. She saw that it was the entrance of a large natural cave, lit by a spluttering pressure-gas lantern. A grubbily dressed peasant woman worked over a stove, and glanced inquisitively at her.

Her captor waved her to sit, and the woman brought her a bowl of strong-smelling fish-stew and a lump of what appeared to be grey putty. This must be the famous *gofio*, Consuelo thought, which she had heard of but never tried;

the maize-dough of the aborigines. On the rough-hewn table
was a greasy spoon.

'I'm not hungry.'

'As you wish,' said the man, 'but you won't get anything
else until the morning.'

She thought she'd better try to eat for her unborn child's
sake, and picked off a piece of the *gofio*, which wasn't unpalat-
able though she thought it would be very indigestible. The
thick soup contained dried cod and cabbage, and its smell
turned her stomach.

'Can I have some water?'

'Here, take some wine,' said the woman. 'The water won't
be safe for you to drink.' She handed her a heavy earthen-
ware jug and a dirty glass.

Consuelo drank a little, and tried a spoonful of the thick
stew, which tasted vile.

'When you've finished, I'll show you your sleeping quarters,' said the man. 'I should warn you that it's impossible to
escape from this valley, especially in your condition, so don't
even consider it, lady.'

'But why have you abducted me and what use am I to
you?'

'It's just orders, lady. It shouldn't be for many days—a
week or so.'

'A week!' expostulated Consuelo. 'I'll be in labour long
before then!'

'Then Catalina here will have to help you when it comes.'

The peasant woman did not look pleased to be cast in the
rôle of midwife, but said nothing.

Her guard pushed open a door made of rough planks and
showed her a *catre* or camp-bed with a wooden frame and
strips of osier that formed the base.

'The woman will bring you a mattress and a couple of
blankets. I'll leave you one candle for the night. There's a
bucket in the corner and a jerry-can of water to wash in.'

The woman brought the bedding and left her a grubby

towel. If only she could get her on her own, thought Consuelo, she might enlist her help to escape. But the woman eyed Consuelo's clothes enviously and stared at her bulging abdomen. She didn't look as though she'd prove to be any kind of ally.

'Can I have my handbag?' Consuelo asked the man.

'It will be brought to you.'

He closed the door on her and she could hear him fixing a strong plank across it between two slots. She was a prisoner, and like all prisoners set out to examine the place where she was to be confined. The room had a ceiling and two walls of dry rock, while the other two walls were of thick planks nailed together, one adjoining the main cave and the other the exterior, to judge by the small window that was boarded up. She peered through the planks on that side but could see nothing in the dark valley outside.

Consuelo hoped that there would be no vermin or bugs, which she abhorred; she'd heard that there were large poisonous lizards in the interior and prayed not to encounter one. In the dim light of the candle she examined the grubby mattress carefully for signs of lice or fleas, and then the blankets. They seemed to be free of infestation. She lay down gingerly on the uncomfortable bed and began to weep silently. It hadn't been exactly the evening she had planned.

Although the plane had left Barajas twenty minutes late, it made its approach over the sea to land at Gando airport almost on time. There must have been a tail wind, thought Bernal. He could see the landing lights now and superstitiously crossed himself as the pilot found the start of the runway right over the rocks at the sea's edge and made a fairly smooth touchdown. When the Boeing had taxied to the terminal building and one of the front doors was opened, the movable gangway was at once wheeled up and Bernal was one of the first to descend.

He made his way to the arrivals hall and, knowing there

would be a delay before the baggage was unloaded, he went to the exit to look for Consuelo. He surveyed the expectant faces of those who were meeting the flight, but couldn't see her among them. The flight being a domestic one there were no passport or customs formalities, so he went out into the car-park to look for her. Still no sign. Perhaps she'd been delayed in the traffic or hadn't felt up to driving. He went to the desk marked INFORMACIÓN and asked the bored girl who was reading the weekly magazine *Diez Minutos* whether there was a message for him.

'I don't think so, sir.' She looked through the pigeonholes in front of her. 'No, sir, I'm afraid not.'

Bernal made for the row of telephones and rang Consuelo's villa.

'Has Señora Lozano left to meet me at the airport, Señorita?'

'*Sí, sí, señor*. Before nine o'clock it was. Isn't she there yet? I've got the dinner on the stove.'

'You'd better turn it off for the time being,' said Bernal. 'She must have had a puncture or a breakdown.'

He went back to the arrivals hall but there was still no sign of Consuelo Lozano. At last the baggage started to emerge along a moving rubber belt and he looked out for his suitcase. He was luckier than usual: it was among the first and was undamaged. He returned to wait at the exit and lit up a Kaiser. Either she would arrive late or a message would come from her, he was sure.

After half an hour he began to get concerned. He decided to have a word with the police authorities at the airport, who would be the Guardia Civil, he realized. On showing the DSE gold star and badge of a *Comisario de primera* he was admitted to the office of the lieutenant in charge. He explained the problem as delicately as he could. Señora Lozano was in the final month of pregnancy; she had arranged to meet his flight and her maid had confirmed that she had left her villa above Las Palmas before 9.0 p.m. If she had had a

puncture or a breakdown, she should have got a message
through by now to the airport or to her maid. But if she
had suffered an accident, or gone into labour, she might not
have been able to do so. Could the lieutenant contact the
hospitals, perhaps?

The lieutenant was eager to help. 'As well as doing that,
Comisario, I'll put out a general call to our Traffic Division,
and to that of the Policía Municipal in Las Palmas. Do you
know what car the Señora was driving?'

'All I know is that it was a hired Renault,' said Bernal, 'but
I could try to find out the details from her maid if I could use
a telephone.'

'It would be useful to find out what she was wearing too,'
added the lieutenant.

All these inquiries were put in hand, and Bernal tried to
calm the maid, Manolita, who became rather hysterical on
the phone.

'Now tell me what the car is like. It's a Renault, isn't it?
Blue? Metallic blue? Do you know what model, Manolita?'

But she knew nothing of these things, and he asked her to
look through Consuelo's papers for the hire agreement.

'I don't think I could, Señor. I'm not sure of papers and
suchlike.'

With sudden insight he realized that she was illiterate, or
nearly so.

'Don't worry, Manolita. I'll come up to the villa and we'll
look for it together.' Bernal turned to the Civil Guard
lieutenant. 'Could you spare a car to take me to the house or
shall I take a taxi?'

'I've got a jeep spare, Superintendent, if you don't mind
being driven in that by one of my men.'

'That will be fine. It's most kind of you.'

On the coastal road to Las Palmas, Bernal looked out for
signs of broken-down blue Renaults. The more he thought
about it, the more alarmed he was becoming. The island was

very thickly populated, with almost three times as many people to the square kilometre as the Peninsula itself, so that it was odd that Consuelo had not been able to contact anyone or send a message. The initial police inquiries had proved fruitless: she hadn't been taken to hospital by ambulance, nor had the police been called to an accident involving her. The breakdown service of the Guardia Civil had not been called to her car. It was possible that a private towing-truck had been contacted, but in that case she would have got to a telephone long since. Bernal had a premonition that something much worse had happened to her, but he couldn't put his finger on the reason for feeling it.

When they reached the pleasant villa, Bernal could see that it commanded a view of the whole length of the city as far as La Isleta, and the sweep of the eastern bay was garlanded by a row of lights that shimmered amber in the dusty night-haze.

It was clear that Manolita the maid had been crying.

'What can have happened to the Señora?' she moaned. 'She went off so happy to meet you, Señor, and look, she'd laid the table so prettily.'

'Now we must keep calm, Manolita, and try to find the car papers to get its number. That way the police will find it quickly.'

The girl got even more upset at this, and Bernal patted her shoulder.

She pointed to a writing-desk in the corner of the living-room. 'That's where the Señora keeps her papers.'

Bernal began to search through the papers while the Civil Guard waited on the porch.

'Give him a beer, Manolita, while I look through these.'

After five minutes he found a receipt from the car hire company and scanned it quickly. Ah, thank goodness, they had put in the *matrícula* as well as the model and year.

'Here it is,' he called out to the guard. 'It's a metallic blue Renault Five with a local registration.'

'I'll radio it through to the Traffic Division, Comisario. They'll put out a general call and it should be spotted quite soon if it's parked in a public place.'

Bernal was not so sanguine about that. In his experience there were always plenty of remote streets where a car could remain for days without the police checking it. Of course it was true that Las Palmas only had 230,000 inhabitants compared with Madrid's almost four million, but Gran Canaria was wild and rugged in its hinterland and cars were easy to hide. But Consuelo shouldn't have departed from the main routes unless she had stopped to buy something.

'Was there anything she said she was going to fetch on her way to the airport, Manolita?' he called out. He noticed that the maid was calmer now that she'd been ogled by the Civil Guard, who was drinking beer out of a can on the verandah.

'She didn't say she was, Señor. She brought champagne and everything earlier.'

Bernal took a sudden decision. 'Would you get my case in from the jeep?' he asked the guard. 'I'll stay here tonight in case the Señora returns, and I'll keep in touch with your lieutenant by phone. Do you know what time he goes off duty?'

'He's on nights this week, Superintendent. He goes off at seven-thirty in the morning.'

Bernal spent a sleepless night in an armchair by the telephone, having persuaded the maid to go to bed, though she swore she wouldn't sleep a wink. Quite soon he could hear her light snoring from the back of the villa. He took a look at all Consuelo's papers to see if he could spot any clues as to the reason for her disappearance. He opened her black briefcase and examined the few papers it contained. They seemed to be photocopies of bank statements on which she had marked certain entries in red ink in the margin.

He tried to make sense of the extracts, but he knew he was no accountant. He'd take them to the bank when it opened in the morning and ask the manager what they were about. As he returned them to the case, he spotted some copies of cancelled cheques made out to Bearer and signed in a rubricated flourish. He tried to decipher the signatures: *Tama* . . . Hadn't Consuelo mentioned a name to him on the phone? *Tamarán?* That was it, and she had talked about a mysterious company she was investigating. If only he could think of its name; it might be important.

Consuelo Lozano had slept very little in her dismal prison and she had risen a number of times imagining that poisonous lizards were descending upon her from the rocky walls. She had spent long hours watching the candle burn down to a stub until it finally guttered out. Towards dawn she fell into an exhausted sleep, only to be awakened soon afterwards by an unfamiliar noise in her ears and some narrow rays of sunlight falling across her face.

She groaned as she tried to shift her bulk from the lumpy mattress, finally succeeding into putting her feet on the uneven rocky floor. It felt hot on the soles of her feet and this puzzled her. Surely not enough sunlight had entered through the slits in the plank wall to warm it up to such a temperature? She bent down and touched it with her hand. It was definitely hot. Could this be live volcanic rock similar to that found in Lanzarote or Tenerife, where lava still flowed from time to time? She had thought that all the cones in Gran Canaria had long been extinct and hadn't erupted at all in historical times. Perhaps the base of this *caldera* was like a geyser or hot water spring, though she could see no sign of moisture in these rocks, which looked smooth as though they had once been molten.

Consuelo listened to the strange whining noise outside, the pitch of it rising and falling, not, she thought, by an increase or diminution in power but by a kind of Doppler effect: whenever the pitch lowered the noise receded from her. She got up and tried to peer through the cracks in the plank wall, but she could only see the shadow of some moving object that crossed the rays of the rising sun from time to time, when it coincided with the rise in pitch of the electronic whine. It was some sort of machine, she was sure, but for the life of her she couldn't guess what kind.

She examined the boarding that had been nailed over the window and attempted to prise out the lowest strip of wood with her bare hands. One side of it felt loose and she decided it would be worth working on if only she had some kind of tool. If her captors left her with some cutlery later on, that might do the trick. Of course she'd been warned that escape was impossible, but they would say that just to discourage her from trying. They'd find that she was made of sterner stuff.

If she could loosen the window-boards and climb out after darkness fell, she might be able to follow the track up to the road and get to the village they had passed about ten minutes before they had arrived in this Godforsaken spot. She reasoned that the truck couldn't have climbed the steep rise above the village and then made the descent into this deep crater at much more than 35 to 40 k.p.h., and most of that part had been taken in second gear. Therefore the village of Valle los Nueves was about five to six km. away. Even in her condition she ought to get there in two hours or so, and if she could put the boards back across the window so that it looked nailed up, they might not notice her escape until first light. By then she'd have got to a telephone.

First, however, she had to get the boards loosened. She looked in her handbag which had been returned to her and searched it for her manicure set. Some of the tools, though small, might be of some use. Blast them! They'd removed it. At least they'd left her lipstick and foundation pack. She looked at her face in the tiny glass in the compact lid and groaned once more: dear God, how ghastly she looked; her hair, which had been expensively set the previous morning, was a disaster after her abduction in the open-sided truck.

She washed herself as best she could in the brackish water in the bucket, then combed her hair and made up her face: at least she'd feel more confident to face whatever the day might bring.

The whining noise outside stopped abruptly and she heard a man shout: 'It's too heavy! It won't work like that!' She hastened back to the boarded-up window, but, frustratingly, the men were out of her line of vision. Oh God, why on earth were they holding her here? What good could it possibly do them? Luis would be out of his mind with worry by now. Suddenly the door burst open behind her and two men in strange uniforms marched in.

Bernal decided that he'd have to go through with his interviews with the civil governor of the province and the head of the Policía Judicial which Paco Navarro had arranged for his first morning. The rest of his group would be arriving that evening, 8 July, which would give them all just ten days to undertake their mission for the Presidency.

More worried than ever by the lack of news about Consuelo, he had telephoned the Civil Guard lieutenant at 7.30 when he was going off duty, but her car had still not been spotted by the night patrols. As soon as the Bank where Consuelo worked opened, he would question the director and find out what accounts Consuelo had been working on.

At 8.30 Bernal rang the Gobernación and left a message to say he would arrive there at 10.30; he wanted to gain some time to search for Consuelo. He told the maid that he would ring her at half-hour intervals in case she received any news, until he had a telephone number at the main *comisaría* to give her. He hoped the police chief would have some offices prepared for them. He would also need transport for himself and his team, preferably unmarked vehicles. At 8.40 he rang for a taxi to take him to the city centre.

The day was grey and cloudy, with the north-east trades still blowing quite strongly. As the flamboyant taxi-driver

sped down the Prolongación de Escaleritas towards the
city, the air got noticeably warmer and muggier. Bernal
pursed his lips and wondered where Consuelo had spent the
night, unless, God forbid, she had suffered a fatal accident.
He tried to shut out the thought. Would he know if she were
in desperate danger by some telepathic message? He had
read of people experiencing such things, but he had never
undergone them nor known anyone who had. Perhaps it was
just an illusion, brought about by a premonition *post eventum*.
More than anything else, he blamed himself; if it weren't for
him, she wouldn't have been out in the Canaries at all.

Now he must spur himself into action. What a pity it was
that his Group wouldn't arrive until the late afternoon, when
they would need some time to install themselves. He decided
to hold an evening briefing, once Paco Navarro had
organized whatever office accommodation the civil governor
and the local Judicial Police intended to put at their disposal.

Bernal ordered the taxi-driver to wait at the Hotel Don
Juan, where he left his suitcase after checking in at Reception
and apologizing for his failure to turn up the previous night.
Then the driver took him the short distance to Mesa y López
and the main office of the Banco Ibérico. Bernal looked at his
watch: 9.05. Quite well timed to see the director just after the
bank opened.

In this he was to be disappointed, as in so many other
matters later on, having forgotten about the slow and
measured way the Canary Islanders normally operated: they
appeared to a brisker person from the Peninsula zombie-like,
aplatanados, as they themselves jokingly referred to their usual
state—'bananaed'—as though the soft and even climate of
the islands made Europe with its constant busyness seem as
remote as the moon. Bernal came to learn that it was no use
berating them: they would turn sullen; so one had to adapt to
their pace which, if slow, was steady and untiring.

Had they always been like this? Bernal wondered; after all,
the *guanches* of Tenerife and the aborigines of Grand Canary

had struck the early European discoverers and settlers as fierce and warlike. Their descendants, however, obviously of mixed blood, seemed listless. Was this the famous *modorra* or wasting disease, or simply the outcome of centuries of external exploitation, with the sad series of briefly successful single-crop economies for which they had naturally provided the labour force? First the wine-trade, then the collection of orchilla-weed for its purple dye; in a later period to-bacco, then bananas, tomatoes and other greenstuff for the European tables, and latterly the tourist industry. The lion's share of the profits had always gone to foreign inter-ests, leaving the indigenous inhabitants as poor as ever. Culturally the islands had never shown much signs of flower-ing in any of the arts; their most famous author, Benito Pérez Galdós, had been just one more successful export. What was characteristic of this friendly and complaisant people was their vast indifference in the face of constant arrivals and departures of foreigners who exhibited the most inexplicable whims, which the islanders fulfilled impassively, without passing judgements.

Bernal lit a Kaiser and, with these reflections, tried to calm his impatience in the waiting-room outside the bank direc-tor's office. Finally a short, fair-haired employee entered to explain that the director wasn't expected at such an early hour, but could the deputy director help the Comisario?

When this official came, Bernal explained that he was concerned about the disappearance the previous evening of Señora Lozano, the director's personal assistant, and told him that the Guardia Civil were actively seeking her hired car after putting out a general alert. Bernal didn't reveal his personal relationship with Consuelo, and began to wonder how he would account for his interest in her to his own team when they arrived.

The deputy director looked suddenly worried and Bernal asked whether Señora Lozano had access to the vault keys.

'We must consider the possibility that she is being held

hostage and that a demand will be made to the bank.'

'But Señora Lozano had no connection with that side of things, Superintendent. She never handled keys or any business to do with the vault or safe deposits.'

'What did her normal duties consist of?'

'She was seconded to us for six months as personal assistant to the director, so that she helped to deal with the affairs of our most important clients.'

'Therefore she had access to information of prime importance to the bank,' Bernal pointed out. 'I take it you have a lot of foreign business, such as transfers of funds in various currencies.'

'That's perfectly true, Superintendent, but I don't really see what her abductors could hope to gain by their action, unless it's going to be a ransom attempt.'

'If that's the case, we'll soon hear from them.'

Bernal showed the deputy director the contents of Consuelo's briefcase.

'Can you recognize from these photocopies what accounts she was working on?'

The deputy examined the copies of the partial bank statements with care and then looked up.

'Unfortunately these are only extracts from much larger statement sheets, Comisario, and the reference numbers at the top edges don't appear. I'll get the head ledger-clerk to look at them, if you agree. He might be able to recall which clients' accounts these belong to.'

'Very well. In the meantime could I see Señora Lozano's work-desk?'

When he had been taken to the room Bernal sat down heavily in Consuelo's chair, emotionally overcome by the faint scent of her Parisian perfume that hung in the air. Then he began to examine the desktop carefully, in particular the notepad by the telephone, the top sheet of which was blank, but he noticed that it bore the faint impressions of earlier messages. Not having any technical aids to hand, he lit a cigarette and puffed on it to acquire sufficient ash, which he then tapped into the clean brass ashtray for it to cool. Crumbling it with the end of a pencil, he tipped the dark powder on to the notepad and blew gently to spread it evenly and remove the excess.

Now he could read some scribbled words in Consuelo's hand: 5.00 h. Ciudad Jardín. Pío XII . . ., followed by some numbers that weren't quite legible. He would need some other way of finding out the exact address. Was this the appointment Consuelo had gone to armed with the papers contained in her attaché-case? But if so, she had reached home safely afterwards and had seen to domestic matters in a perfectly normal way, according to her maid, until she had left to meet him at Gando airport just before 9.0 p.m. Yet she had not reached the airport, or, if she had, she'd been snatched away before he had arrived. And her car was not parked there; the Civil Guard lieutenant had searched the airport precincts for it as soon as its registration-number had become known. The problem was that the earlier appointment Consuelo had kept might have no direct connection with her disappearance.

Bernal opened the drawers of her desk one by one and looked over the contents. The chief item of interest turned out to be a telex message, dated the previous morning, despatched by the Crédit Français in Paris. As far as Bernal's very limited knowledge of French went, it seemed to refer to regular monthly payments in French francs transmitted from their branch at Algiers and transferred to Gran Canaria in pesetas to the credit of Alcorán S.A. Wasn't that name familiar to him for some reason? Hadn't he read it or seen it very recently?

Picking up the alphabetical volume of the local telephone directory, Bernal looked up the name of the firm, but it wasn't listed. That struck him as very curious, unless, of course, the company's office wasn't in Las Palmas, but in that case why was the money regularly transferred to this branch of the Banco Ibérico? Having found nothing else of interest, or at least that made any sense to him, Bernal determined to ask the deputy director to re-examine all the contents of the desk to see if he could spot anything out of the ordinary.

Just then that official entered, accompanied by another employee.

'This is our chief ledger-clerk, Comisario. As you will probably realize, we don't have ledgers nowadays but keep all our statements and files on the main computer, from which we print hard copy as required. It's likely that these sheets you found in Señora Lozano's briefcase were made on one of our Xerox copying machines on A4 paper from originals which consist of much wider fanfold sheets, vulgarly called *papel pijama* because of the green stripes. Look, you can just make them out in the shading on these photocopies.'

'What about the red marks Señora Lozano has put against certain entries?'

The ledger-clerk now spoke up. 'They reveal a disturbing state of affairs, Superintendent. It appears that a large sum is being recycled every month through various subsidiary accounts to give the appearance of credit balances from time to time, and Señora Lozano spotted this.'

'But can you identify the account-holders?' asked Bernal.

'I probably will be able to from the dates shown on these entries, by checking with the daily transaction lists, but it will take time.'

'Perhaps there's a quicker way,' Bernal commented, producing from his pocket the telex message he had found in Consuelo's desk. 'Tell me what you think about this.'

The ledger-clerk and the deputy manager pored over the message.

'Alcorán S.A.,' commented the clerk. 'I'll check at once to see if we have accounts in the name of such a firm.'

He switched on a VDU connected with the main computer and began tapping the controls.

'What happens if there's a power cut or some damage occurs to the computer?' Bernal asked the deputy manager. 'Would the bank lose its records?'

'We take precautions against all that, Comisario. We keep in the vault hard-disk copies of all the transactions made each day, and much of the information is made available on paper print-outs. The most important thing is the security of access to the main computer which connects to our head-quarters in Madrid and via there to all our branches. We have to watch out for "hackers" who might try to gain illegal access to it to pay themselves unauthorized sums. The computer manufacturers provide security codes and devices which are changed daily.'

'Yet such computer frauds are becoming commonplace in banking circles, aren't they?' commented Bernal. 'We've had to set up a special group to cope with it in the Policía Judicial.'

'Not here in Las Palmas, thank goodness!' the deputy said, smiling. 'Or not yet, at any rate.'

The ledger-clerk called them to the computer terminal.

'Alcorán S.A. has accounts with us, Comisario. Here on the screen you can see the latest movements in their current account and part of it coincides with one of the extracts Señora Lozano was using.'

'What's the address of the company?' asked Bernal anxiously.

The clerk tapped more keys. 'Here it is, Comisario. Calle Pío XII, 112, in the Ciudad Jardín suburb.'

'Ah, I think we're getting somewhere,' said Bernal with no little satisfaction. 'Is there a phone number?'

The clerk wrote it down for him.

'Would you ring the number?' Bernal asked the deputy director. 'Please ask if they had a visit from Señora Lozano yesterday at five o'clock.'

The deputy dialled the number and let the ringing tone go on for some minutes, but then shook his head.

'They're not answering this morning, Superintendent.'

Consuelo turned rapidly away from the boarded-up window of her prison when she heard the door slam open. She was astonished to see Señor Tamarán and a tall Arab-looking man she hadn't seen earlier, both dressed in camouflaged flak-jackets and black berets.

'Why have you had me abducted and brought here?' she demanded.

'You brought it on yourself, Señora,' said Tamarán coldly. 'If you hadn't been so inquisitive about our affairs . . .'

'But you've absolutely no right to do this to me,' broke in Consuelo, fuming. 'Do you realize the seriousness of your crime if anything happens to me or to my child? All I've done is no more than my duty to the bank. Your firms are committing a fraud.'

'It's too late for all this, Señora. We must hold you as our prisoner for another ten days. Then you'll be set free as soon as we're in charge.'

'In charge of what, for Heaven's sake?' she asked angrily. 'The Civil Guard must be searching for me already.'

'They'll never find you down here, so you'll have to make the best of it. I've ordered them to bring you a better bed and more comfortable things. The woman will look after you.'

'And has she experience as a midwife too?' asked Consuelo icily. 'My child is due on the eighteenth and I could go into labour sooner than that. I should be in the maternity wing of the hospital some days before, because it's my first child. You'll be held responsible if anything goes wrong.'

'It's all your own fault,' retorted Tamarán angrily. 'In any case, who will there be to hold me responsible? We shall be running everything by then in all the islands.'

Consuelo noticed that his companion had said nothing throughout the exchanges and looked at her impassively as though he understood little of what had been said. Was he an Arab or a Berber? she wondered.

'Running everything in these islands?' she gasped in reply. 'But that's impossible and you know it is. The Government has the whole of the Legion out here, as well as the army training camps and the airforce base at Gando. How can you take over all that?' she said in a pitying tone in order to provoke him into an indiscretion.

Tamarán got angrier. 'You and your friends will soon get a taste of the strength of our forces for the liberation of the Canaries from the Spanish yoke. Our Saharan allies will help us win the day.'

So that was it, Consuelo thought. The other man must be from the Western Sahara where she knew a guerrilla campaign was still being waged against the Moroccan army since Spain had given up its old African possession.

'Now I advise you to cooperate with us, Señora,' Tamarán went on in a more menacing tone, 'that is if you want to celebrate Liberation Day with us.'

Suddenly from outside there came the loud whirring of helicopters approaching, and Tamarán plus his companion made a rapid exit, shutting and bolting the door after them. Consuelo rushed to the window and tried as hard as she could to prise open one of the boards to see what was happening. She was surprised when she glimpsed through the crack four large transport helicopters bellying down in a cloud of yellow dust on the floor of the *caldera*, and then four platoons of troops clambering down from them and lining briskly up for inspection. They looked young and well disciplined.

Tamarán and his henchman went over to them and Consuelo strained to see how they saluted him. Clearly he was the leader, or at least the local leader, of these mercenaries or whatever they were who were planning a *coup de main*. She watched the four helicopters take off again in a huge flurry of dust and turn towards the east as they rose up out of the volcanic crater, but she couldn't make out any markings on the brown-painted machines.

Later, from her difficult lookout position, she saw khaki field-tents being pitched under the lee of the high rocky cliffs towards the northern end of the *caldera*, judging by the angle of the morning sun. Again she tugged at the partly loosened board to see if it would come free but her bare hands would not serve. When next they brought her food, she would try to keep back a piece of cutlery to have some sort of implement. All at once she felt the child move within her, and she had to double up on the creaky and uncomfortable camp-bed to obtain an easier posture. Oh God, she thought, what if the contractions start in earnest in this forlorn spot, without any prospect of medical assistance?

Superintendent Bernal took another taxi from the Banco Ibérico to the Garden City suburb of Las Palmas, which was on the way to his chief destination at the civil governor's headquarters where he was due at 10.30 a.m. He asked the driver to wait for him outside the office-block in Pío XII, where he checked the address of Alcorán S.A. on the index-board in the cool marble hallway, there being no porter visible in the lodge. After calling the lift, he was borne swiftly up to the fifth floor, where he found the landing deserted, but the glass doors of the offices of Alcorán S.A. ajar.

Bernal entered silently and stopped to listen. He observed signs of a hasty departure at the receptionist's desk, some drawers of which were tipped out on to the floor. He tried the door of what appeared to be the main office and it opened with a slight creak. The room was unoccupied and again indicated that there had been a hurried removal. The desk and filing cabinet yawned open, and he made a rapid search to see if anything had been overlooked, but he found nothing. Bernal left the room quietly and explored the long corridor with caution. Suddenly he glimpsed a door being opened slowly at the far end, and he clutched instinctively for his police-issue pistol which made a thick bulge inside his lightweight mohair suit.

A small middle-aged man dressed in denims emerged and looked at him without appearing at all surprised: 'What a mess they've left! And I'm the one who'll be expected to clean it up! Are you from the property agency?'

'Are you the caretaker?' asked Bernal, without answering the question.

'That's right. All the work always falls on me. Just look at these coils of wires they've left and the marks on the walls.' He beckoned Bernal to inspect the room he had just come out of. 'The landlord will send them a hefty bill for all this, that's for sure.'

Bernal examined the windowless room, empty now except for a complex jumble of electrical cables still attached to the points in the skirting-board. He noted that some thicker brown cable penetrated the wall to the exterior.

'Was there a window here once?'

'There was, but they blocked it up. That'll cost them a bit to put right, I can tell you.'

'What time did they move out?'

'A big furniture-van arrived soon after seven o'clock this morning and they began taking all those electronic machines out. I watched to make sure they didn't take any of the furniture that goes with this suite of offices.'

'Did they leave any forwarding address for the mail and so on?'

'No, they didn't, 'cause I asked them specially.' The porter suddenly became alarmed. 'Didn't they tell the agent's office?'

Bernal showed the man his official Superintendent's gold badge and explained that he was anxious to track down the directors of Alcorán S.A.

'I only hope I don't get the blame. They said they'd paid the rent for six months in advance and they've only been here for four months. I'd better ring up the agency.'

'You can do that in a minute. First show me where these brown wires lead.'

'Up to the roof, which is still festooned with their aerials.' The porter led the way towards the lift. 'The woman who lives in the attic apartment was so mad with them for messing up the flat roof. She can't hang her washing out properly, she says, and the aerials hummed when they were using the machines, so that she thought she'd be electrocuted. Very unpleasant lot of people they were, too.'

'Did you notice the name of the firm on the removals van?'

'It was one of those large hired transit vans, with no name on the sides.'

The porter showed Bernal the way on to the flat roof that ran round four sides of the well of the interior patio of the seven-storey building, from where they had a splendid view of the palm-lined bay under the white light filtered by the thin cloud-layer.

'These are the aerials they put up, Superintendent.'

The top-floor tenant who had been so put out by the festooned wires now emerged from her roof-dwelling when she saw them and began to harangue the porter.

'Oy, aren't they coming back to take all these monstrosities away? I'm sick and tired of having all this stuff up here.'

'They didn't say, Sagrario, but if they don't, I'll get on to the landlord about it.'

Bernal inspected the large metal structures and decided that they were much more than aerials: the central poles with complex dipoles looked to him much more like transmitters, which were directed towards the north-east.

'I'll send a technician to look at all this equipment,' he told the porter. 'In the meantime, lock this door that leads on to the roof. If anyone from Alcorán S.A. comes back, telephone me at once at the Policía Judicial building. Don't give them the keys, mind.'

When they descended in the lift, Bernal asked to be let out

again at the fifth floor in order to make a further search of the
abandoned offices.

He explored the grey filing cabinets to see if any documents had slipped to the bottom of a drawer and been
overlooked. The search drew a blank until he turned to the
receptionist's desk in the hallway. There, caught between the
upper and lower drawers he found a carbon copy of a letter
dated the previous day and addressed to a Señor Mencey,
Avenue Lafayette, Algiers. He tucked it thoughtfully into his
breast-pocket, and finding nothing else of interest made his
way down to the street to look for a taxi to take him to the
Gobierno Civil building in the Plaza del Ingeniero León y
Castillo.

As the morning passed slowly, much too slowly, for Consuelo
Lozano, she found she got more relief from her discomfort by
lying flat on the rocky floor of her cell, which was peculiarly
hot to the touch, so much so that she had spread the worn
goat's-hair blanket they had given her to line it. She had
spent at least an hour watching through the cracks in the
boarding the strangely clad troops who had arrived in the
helicopters settling in their field-tents at the other side of the
volcanic floor of the *caldera*.

Now from where she lay she could hear the echoes of their
coarse laughter and smell the woodsmoke from the camp-
fires lit by the cooks who had began to prepare some kind of
stew in large cooking-pots. Earlier she had caught glimpses
of them chopping up meat on a flat rock.

Consuelo began to get drowsy from the unusual warmth of
the cave and finally dozed off, dreaming that she was on a
flat-bottomed boat which swayed from side to side as it was
borne along on a fiery stream; the craft suddenly descended
through terrifying rapids of molten lava from which fierce
sparks rose and spat at her. She woke with a start, bathed in
perspiration, feeling the ground pitching beneath her, and
she clutched at the leg of the truckle-bed for safety. What a

silly dream, she thought, pulling her great weight on to the
grimy mattress. Her head swayed with dizziness and she
held on tight to the bed. She must be suffering from a
nauseous faint, which the doctor had warned her about.

Suddenly she could hear shouts of alarm from the soldiers,
and a curious creaking from the boards of her prison. She
struggled to open her eyes which had become sensitive to the
light, and sat up on the unstable bed.

The taxi left Bernal at the steps that led up to the imposing
building of the Gobierno Civil, where he presented his
credentials and asked to be taken to the Civil Governor's
office. He was five minutes early for his appointment. A very
decorative ash-blonde secretary ushered him to a low settee
in the waiting-room and went off to inform the Governor
of his arrival. She soon reappeared and led him to His
Excellency's presence.

On entering the large, cool, sunlit office, Bernal at first
could see no one.

'Come over here, Comisario. I'm so glad you've arrived,'
said a voice that arose from behind the large ornate
desk.

Bernal peered over the desk and found the Civil Governor
kneeling on the floor in front of a large-scale plan of Las
Palmas which was fully unrolled and held down by heavy
books at the corners.

Bernal shook hands awkwardly, and squatted at the
Governor's side.

'I was appalled to see that the detailed routes of the
President's visit were given in yesterday's *Canarias 7*, Your
Excellency. That kind of publicity endangers security and
makes our task much harder.'

'It didn't leak from this office, Comisario. It was the Press
office in Madrid. They gave it out to the national news
agency without telling us they were going to.'

'What about the President's visit to Tenerife and La

Gomera? Have the detailed timings of that visit been released too?'

'The whole shoot, I'm sorry to say.'

'We'd better consider how some of the timings and routes can be changed, Excellency, in order to throw any potential terrorists off the scent. Have your local people reported any threats?'

'Nothing so far. Of course they've started a twenty-four-hour watch on known subversives.'

'Perhaps you'd be so kind as to take me over the plans as they now stand, Excellency.'

'Well, as you know, it's just a one-and-a-half-day visit, Comisario. The President flies in at sixteen-hundred hours on the seventeenth from Reina Sofía airport in Tenerife. I'll be meeting him at Gando, accompanied by representatives of the Cabildo Insular and a guard of honour drawn from the Las Palmas barracks. Then he'll be driving with me in the official car to this building to greet the local government officials. After that I'll take him up to my official residence where he'll be staying before leaving for Fuerteventura. After a brief rest and change of clothes he'll be going at eighteen-hundred hours to the Parque Doramas, where he'll first address a meeting of party organizers and election agents in the Hotel Santa Catalina and then attend a display of island folk-dancing in the Pueblo Canario. All this will be followed by a dinner given by the party in the same hotel.'

Bernal looked carefully at the large-scale plan. 'So from six p.m. until about eleven the President will be inside the Parque Doramas, where presumably you will have ordered tight security.'

'My people have it all in hand, Comisario. Special passes for all personnel and the guests, a complete search of the grounds with sniffer dogs, metal-detectors at the main entrance and so on.'

'What about the route to and from your official residence? How will that be covered?'

'The usual precautions: a search of the bridges on the route an hour before the official car is due, policemen at every road-junction to close off traffic five minutes before we get there, police sharpshooters on the rooftops and high points.'

'And the next day, the eighteenth?' asked Bernal, looking again at the map. 'It's an important anniversary, when extremists might come out in force.'

'It's especially important here in Las Palmas, Comisario.' The Civil Governor smiled faintly. 'You know that when I was a teenager I saw Franco making his *pronunciamiento* from the Cabildo building in July 1936 before that English pilot flew him from the old airfield to North Africa ready to launch his invasion of the Peninsula.'

'Many others of different political persuasions will remember it too,' commented Bernal. 'Let's hope they don't try to imitate it in some way. What is the President's schedule on the morning of the eighteenth?'

'Before his address to the Island Council in the Cabildo building at eleven, he'll drive to the port to inaugurate the new oil terminal.'

'That's going to be the riskiest part of the visit,' said Bernal, examining the plan carefully. 'You'll have to take him along the entire length of the Avenida Marítima and then negotiate the narrow streets of the isthmus in order to get to the commercial port.'

'El Refugio, Superintendent, that's what we call the narrow part, where our ancestors used to take refuge behind a stockade from the fierce aborigines. But the police have it all in hand. The buildings giving on to the route will all be searched from eight-hundred hours, the rooftops manned with armed guards and the streets lined with police. The official Mercedes is bullet-proof, so it would take a large bomb to blow us up.'

'Don't forget that was exactly what happened to Admiral Carrero Blanco in Madrid in 1973,' remarked Bernal. 'Have you ordered a search of the sewers and soundings to be taken of the roadway in case anyone has tunnelled under it?'

'That's a good point, Bernal. I'll order it to be done the day before the visit.'

'I suggest your men make an initial inspection today on all the routes, Excellency. That kind of subversive plan needs a lot of preparation.' Bernal pointed to the routes marked on the plan in red. 'Couldn't we alter the programme for the eighteenth and put the opening of the oil terminal after the address to the Cabildo Insular?'

'But all the invitations have been sent out, Comisario. It would cause a lot of headaches if we changed round the ceremonies now.'

'In that case a change of route would be a good idea. I see there are two roads leading across the isthmus from the city to the port. Why don't you switch to the more westerly road?'

'But Albareda is a much wider street and to get into the more westerly one, Sagasta, would entail entering a maze of side-streets near the Parque de Santa Catalina. In any case, once we reach the Calle de Juan Rejón and the Castillo de la Luz there's really no other way to reach the oil terminal.'

'That's the part that worries me most, Excellency. Had you considered using a helicopter?'

'The Military Governor is against it, Comisario, and I understand the President himself dislikes riding in choppers.'

By lunch-time Bernal had made a few more minor suggestions for improving security during the President's visit, and then inspected the suite of offices placed at the disposal of his group at the Policía Judicial headquarters. The Superintendent-in-charge treated him with exquisite courtesy, almost exaggerated deference, thought Bernal, but seemed to be under the delusion that the temporary secondment of Bernal's Group from Madrid was little more than a formal gesture on the Government's part. He appeared very surprised, therefore, when Bernal asked to see copies of all the police incident reports for the previous fortnight.

'Of course I'll have them sent over to you, Comisario, but they'll make a large pile of paper for you to go through.'

'I always think it best to start with all the paper one can get, Superintendent,' said Bernal. 'Small details stick in one's mind which may acquire great importance later on.' He looked round the comfortable but bare office that had been provided. 'Could we have some large wall-charts of the whole island and of the city with the President's routes marked on them?'

'I'll put it in hand, Comisario.'

As soon as he was alone, Bernal telephoned the Civil Guard lieutenant at Gando airport to find out if he had any news of Consuelo, whose disappearance left him feeling sick and unable to think clearly.

'I regret to say we still haven't found her blue Renault, Superintendent, which must be seen as a good sign, don't you think? It may be that she drove to some remote spot to get something we don't know about and then got stuck there far from a telephone.'

Bernal suspected that the lieutenant was being deliberately over-optimistic in order to reassure him.

'Let's face it, Lieutenant; fifteen hours have gone by since she was last seen. Whatever you imagine she may have gone to obtain, where is there so remote that she couldn't have got help to send us a message by now, if she's well and ablebodied?'

He listened carefully to the lieutenant's suggestion.

'There are some places on the coast, Comisario, en route to the airport at Gando, where they sell fresh fish and shellfish. She may have gone to one of them after hearing about it from somebody local, especially if she found she had time in hand, in order to get a speciality for the table.'

'But her maid has attested to the fact that Señora Lozano did the shopping yesterday on her way home, including a purchase of fresh prawns.'

'Well, if it wasn't food, it could have been something else. Now there's the small town of Telde, I hadn't thought of that before. It's the old island town, by-passed by the new coast road, a place where the tourists hardly ever go. It has a lot of shops specializing in local handicrafts that the dealers frequent. Telde's not far from the airport.'

'But would she have gone there after nine p.m. when the shops would have been closed?' asked Bernal doubtfully. But he didn't want to discourage the officer from greater efforts. 'Send your men to search there in any case, Lieutenant. One never knows with pregnant women; they get peculiar whims.' Bernal tried to sound encouraging. 'By the way, did you get my message earlier this morning about that mysterious firm Alcorán S.A. whose financial affairs Señora Lozano was investigating for the Banco Ibérico? They did an early-morning flit from their offices in Pío XII.'

'I'm cooperating with the Policía Nacional in tracking down their new whereabouts, Comisario.'

'Give it your urgent attention, Lieutenant. I don't think their move was coincidental. My instincts warn me that they may have abducted Señora Lozano in order to keep her silent about their financial affairs.'

Consuelo Lozano managed to struggle to her feet when she heard the woman shouting from the larger part of the cavern. Staggering across to the boarded-up window, Consuelo craned her neck to see what was causing alarm among the soldiers. She managed to make out a crowd of them between the field-tents and the large rock where the cooks had chopped up the meat and lit their camp-fires, and some of them were backing off in fright from a huge cloud of steam emerging from a hole in the rocky floor of the *caldera*.

Consuelo clutched at the slightly loosened board and she was delighted to find it fell away in her hand. Whatever had happened, it had been sufficient to move a piece of the boarding. She heard the door being opened and hastily tried to put the board back into place so that her captors would not notice it.

The slovenly woman entered and beckoned her out. 'You'd better come with me.'

'What is it? What's wrong?'

'It's Alcorán, he's whispering to us. It's a bad sign; mark my words.'

Consuelo felt confused. 'Alcorán? But that's Señor Tamarán's firm, isn't it?'

The woman looked at her blankly. 'It's Alcorán, the god of the mountains. He's just spat at us. That's molten lava those men are running away from out there.'

'But the volcano hasn't been active here for hundreds of years, has it?' asked Consuelo worriedly. 'I thought the only activity in modern times was in Tenerife, Lanzarote and La Palma.'

'We've often seen these small break-outs up here in the hills. They don't know or care about it down there in the city. When I was a girl I remember quite a quake in Nieves.'

'But aren't we in danger?' asked Consuelo, looking out at the towering clouds of steam.

'I shouldn't think so. The old gods are a bit angry, that's what I think.' She crossed herself superstitiously and kissed a silver pendant she wore. 'What you can see is just steam from the water under the floor of this *hoyo*. Those dirty Africans haven't seen such a thing before, that's all.'

This was the longest speech Consuelo had ever heard the woman make in her thick, almost impenetrable hinterland accent. If she disapproved of the African intruders, perhaps she could be won over to assist in an escape attempt.

'Do you know why they're holding me prisoner?' Consuelo began tentatively. 'My baby's due in a few days time and it's my first. I really ought to be in the maternity hospital.'

The old woman chuckled. 'I've lost count of how many I had, what with so many miscarriages. I had my first on the beach in a thunderstorm with only my younger sister to help me, and she was terrified out of her silly wits. My mother didn't know I was expecting, you see.'

'What happened to the baby?' asked Consuelo in horrified fascination.

'Oh, we buried it among the rocks at low tide. It was stillborn.' The woman sighed heavily. 'It was just as well, since I didn't know for sure who its father was.' She suddenly let out a cackle. 'I was only fourteen then, and the civil war was on. There were a lot of legionaries about here then.'

They could hear a louder hiss from the escaping steam and Consuelo looked anxiously out.

'Will we be safe in this cave? The floor seems to be awfully hot.'

'Of course we will. This has been used for generations by my people. And there are a lot more like this further up the cliff. Our ancestors used to mummify the dead and put them in these places with food and drink for their eternal journey.'

Consuelo looked about her with a horrified shudder.

'Don't worry,' said the old crone, 'this large cave used to be the *argodey* or place where they honoured the virgin priestesses.' She cackled again. 'A fine pair of virgin priestesses you and me make!'

At 2.0 p.m. that day Bernal sent out for a *bocata* of ham and cheese and a bottle of the local La Tropical beer, for he was anxious not to lose any time for a rapid read of all the recent police incident reports. He noticed from the daily abstracts that most of the reports had been sent in by the Miller Bajo *comisaría,* which had the notorious Catalina Park in its ambit, and by the station at San Agustín, which covered the tourist beaches of Playa del Inglés and Maspalomas.

He made brief notes in his tiny and careful handwriting of the classes of offence that had led to detective inquiries or arrests, which were principally of illicit drug-trafficking, knifings, muggings, break-ins, confidence tricks and contraband—all of them probably routine throughout the year.

He noted that during the previous fifteen days there had occurred only one suspected homicide, no abductions and no political arrests, so that Consuelo's enforced disappearance, if that what it was, would be entirely unusual. He paid special attention to reports about missing persons, of whom there were only five, and three had already been found. There remained the case of a young girl from Arucas and an old man at Mogan.

The most interesting cases of all had been reported by Inspector Guedes of Miller Bajo station and Bernal determined to seek an interview with him as soon as he could about the cadaver discovered at Confital Bay and the woman discovered unconscious in the Calle del Coronel Rocha. Bernal had pored over the large street-plan of Las Palmas that had been brought to his temporary office and had observed that the two cases had occurred in the same district: the unidentified male corpse had been spotted among the rocks below the Isleta quarter not far from where the woman had been found lying. Bernal supposed that Guedes would have guessed there was a connection, or would he? A local officer very familiar with his small patch might well not consult a large-scale plan of the entire city and might therefore miss the comparative proximity of the two cases, given his narrow frame of reference. After all, unconscious people were found in the Santa Catalina square district most nights, in a drunken or drugged state. But this poor, middle-aged woman had turned up in a deserted, almost uninhabited spot, where the ordinary petty criminals of the port were hardly likely to climb. He would mention his intuitive feel about the two cases to the local inspector.

But were these two strange cases likely to have any implications for the Presidential visit? Perhaps they were part of some domestic tragedy—the commonest cause of crime—or even the result of local gang-warfare. As he came wearily to the end of the very large pile of files at almost six o'clock, Bernal was delighted to see Paco Navarro enter his

office accompanied by two more of his inspectors, Miranda
and Lista.

'Thank goodness you're here at last, Paco! I was beginning
to think I was taking over the policing of the island single-
handed.'

'We've just left our bags at the hotel, *jefe*, and come
straight here to set up the office.'

'Where are Ángel and Elena?' asked Bernal.

'Elena insisted on unpacking and hanging up her considerable wardrobe in the Hotel Don Juan, while Ángel said
he'd go back for her after checking into the Tigaday which is
around the corner. He knows his way about because he's
been here on holiday a couple of times.'

'I'll bet he does!' exclaimed Bernal. 'We'll have to keep a
sharp eye on him with all the exotic temptations.'

Bernal pointed to the large-scale plan of the city, with the
President's routes shown in different coloured ribbons and
markers indicating the dates and times.

'I've got the detailed printed schedules from the Civil
Governor, and his security people have taken steps to check
the buildings and the guest-lists at each function. The three
of you had better familiarize yourselves with the arrangements. I'm somewhat concerned about the release of the
details in the local Press, which will give plenty of notice to
any potential subversives. I've already recommended a
number of changes in the routes and the timings, but the
Governor is resisting a bit.'

'What are all these files, chief?' asked Miranda, pointing
at Bernal's desk.

'The incident reports for the past fortnight from the entire
island. I've spent five hours looking for anything unusual
among them.' He indicated a handful of blue files he had put
to one side. 'Perhaps you and Carlos would have a look at
those first, while I fill Paco in about the visit arrangements.
Then I'll want you, Juan, to accompany me to Tomás Miller
police station to see Inspector Guedes. Would you ring him

to make an appointment for us to go there early this evening? Perhaps he'll take us over the ground, which I always prefer to see for myself.'

In his private office, Bernal showed Navarro a very thin file he had kept in a drawer.

'This is something of a personal matter, Paco. It concerns the disappearance yesterday night of Consuelo Lozano, who is an old friend of mine from Madrid. She had invited me to dine and had arranged to meet me at Gando airport, but she never showed up and her car is also missing. I've started a Civil Guard inquiry and I've visited the Banco Ibérico where she worked. It seems from what I've found out that she may have been abducted by a mysterious company called Alcorán S.A. whose shady financial dealings she was investigating.'

'Is there any security angle in it, *jefe*?'

'I didn't think so at first, until I found this telex in her desk at the bank.'

Navarro read through the message about the transfer of funds through the Crédit Français, and looked up at his chief in puzzlement.

'I don't see any connection with the President's security, *jefe*.'

'It's the mention of Algiers, from where the large sums come each month, don't you see? The Canaries separatists have always found a safe hideaway there, even in Franco's time. They could be up to something here and now.'

The two Civil Guards in the green-painted jeep drove slowly along the dusty side-streets of Telde, looking at all the parked vehicles as they passed.

'I think it's a wild-goose chase,' said one to the other gloomily, biting the end off a cheap Canary cigar. 'What would a well-to-do bank employee like this Señora Lozano have been up to in a place like this?'

'Perhaps she had a secret date,' the younger man suggested with a knowing smile.

'But the lieutenant said she was nearly nine months' gone. She wouldn't be much of a thrill for any boyfriend.'

They reached the last outpost of the old town on the southern side, where the broken asphalt of the roadway petered out into volcanic rocks and dust beyond the last of the mean one-storey dwellings.

'Let's turn here,' said the older man, 'and get back to the airport. I could do with a coffee before we go off duty.'

As he swung the steering-wheel to do a U-turn on the stretch of waste ground, the enormous red ball of the setting sun struck them full in the face. When he paused, momentarily blinded, the older Civil Guard said: 'There's a blue car parked over there at the side of the last house. Let's take a look.'

Having been allocated an official car by the local superintendent-in-charge, Bernal ordered the driver to take him and Lista to Miller Bajo *comisaría* in the port area, where Inspector Guedes received them affably.

'I understand you're with us because of the Presidential visit, Comisario. It's a great honour to have you working here.'

'I've skimmed through the incident reports, Guedes, and my eye was caught by two cases you're investigating, though I've no real grounds for thinking they have any security implications. It's just a hunch.'

'You mean the drowned man found at Las Canteras beach, Comisario?'

'Yes, that's one of them. The other is the woman found unconscious up at La Isleta. Has she recovered consciousness?'

'Not again. She has been able to utter only a few words: *Rosario* and *Pardilla*, and ask about her husband, whom we can't trace yet. I'm keeping a series of my men at her bedside in case she comes round, but the doctors think there's no hope for her. We've searched through the entire electoral register for her name, but there's no Rosario Pardilla listed. I've also put in a request to the Documento Nacional de Identidad in Madrid to check on the national computer records. We've taken her fingerprints so as to be able to compare them with the official files if they can turn something up.'

'Look, Guedes, the sun hasn't set yet and I always like to go over the ground myself. Would you show Lista and me the place where she was found? That is if you're not due to go off duty yet.'

'It's so busy in this station that I don't get much time off, Comisario.' Guedes smiled gently. 'Of course I'll take you up there.'

'We'll go in the posh Mercedes they've put at my disposal,' said Bernal. 'I'll read your detailed report on the way.'

As they were driven through the Calle de Sagasta across 'El Refugio', the low cloud that had hung over the capital all day quickly dispersed with the offshore evening breeze, revealing a golden sunset. The driver sped up the Calle del Faro and at the top Guedes ordered him to stop at the corner of Coronel Rocha. When they got out, the local inspector pointed to the row of deserted hovels in the abandoned street nearby.

'That's where the patrol found her early yesterday morning, Comisario. Later I made a search of these houses, and I'm sure this third house was somehow involved. Just there on the doorstep I found the broken pieces of light polished wood that correspond to the fragment the woman was clutching when she was discovered. I put a seal on the door.' He checked to see if it was still intact.

Bernal asked the driver if he had a torch. When it was brought, Guedes broke the seal and they entered the malodorous dwelling.

'There's still a faint smell of kerosene,' commented Bernal.

'It was much stronger yesterday,' said Guedes.

Bernal, watched by Lista and the local inspector, moved the torch's beam slowly over the refuse and broken furniture in the large room of the one-storey building, and suddenly brought it to a stop over a rectangular outline on the dusty stone floor, surrounded by small pools of a dark liquid. Bernal stooped to take a little on to his index finger and sniffed at it.

'Do you think some machine stood here, such as a small portable generator?' he asked. He bent down again to examine some slices of blue, red and brown cable, and asked Lista for a plastic bag to preserve them in. 'It's clear some electrical machinery was used here, and since there isn't any mains supply in these old cottages, they must have used a generator. Now what did they want it for?'

As he and Lista began to move metre by metre across the littered floor, Bernal picked up some flat pieces of lacquered matchwood.

'There may be prints on these,' he commented, holding them by the outer edges. 'You'd better get some string and hang them in a cardboard box not to smudge any latents there may be.' Bernal looked round the rest of the room almost in despair. 'There's really too much evidence, Guedes, and most of it is probably irrelevant since there are months or even years of débris in here. We'll have to guess which is the most recent and try to make some sense of it.'

'That door leads to the back yard, which is also full of garbage,' said Guedes.

With a handkerchief wrapped round his right hand, Bernal lifted the wooden bar that held the battered door in place and pulled the door open by its upper corner. He saw that it opened on to the rising cliff of volcanic rock. He noticed a rusty kerosene can near the doorstop and shook it gently. A few drops appeared to remain inside. He eyed with interest the large oxydized oil-drum that was half-full of dirty water.

'Did you probe to the bottom of this drum?' he asked
Guedes.

'No,' said the local inspector quietly. 'I didn't think of
that.'

'Well, there may be nothing in it of importance, but it's
worth doing. We'll have to take a sample of this water for the
lab to test and then the drum can be tipped out. We'd better
leave a full inspection until first light tomorrow.'

Bernal cast his eye with apparent casualness over the
mounds of extraneous rubbish that spilled on to the rocks.
'You'll need a whole team to sort through all that and they'd
better wear protective clothing and masks. It doesn't look too
salubrious,' he ended, looking in distaste at the small dried
piles of human excrement on which bluebottles buzzed.

Then he looked back at the roof of the hovel which was
caught by the low angle of the setting sun.

'Did you examine those thick brown cables?' he asked
Guedes.

The local inspector looked crestfallen. 'I didn't notice
them, since it was nearly dark when I got here yesterday.'

Guedes stood on an upturned rusty oil-drum and reached
up to the bottom edge of the cable.

'It looks like part of an aerial lead, judging by its gauge,
and there are recent marks of brackets on the stone chimney,
Comisario.'

'Strange, isn't it?' commented Bernal. 'An abandoned
hovel which never had an electricity supply, yet someone had
installed and has recently removed an aerial from its roof.
Whoever it was went to the lengths of bringing in a portable generator to drive some kind of machinery. Hardly a
television set, I wouldn't have thought.'

Guedes shrugged his shoulders and spread out his hands
in a gesture of puzzlement. 'This whole quarter has been
scheduled for demolition for some years now. I can't imagine
what they'd be doing up here.'

Bernal shielded his eyes against the red glow of the setting sun and looked at the sparse landscape with care.

'The one advantage of the spot is the tremendous view. I suppose you could see Tenerife on a clear day.'

'And the African coast and any vessels approaching the port of Las Palmas,' confirmed Guedes.

The three of them looked down on the main quays and the long breakwater of the Puerto de la Luz to the south-east of where they stood, noticing the half-dozen ships berthed there, and beyond them the gleaming metal structures of the new oil terminal below the cliff of El Nido.

'I take it that's what the President will be going to inaugurate?' asked Bernal.

'That's it, Comisario,' said Guedes. 'It's taken two years to build the new terminal at the point of La Isleta furthest from the town in case of explosions.'

Bernal looked away in the opposite direction to the Bay of Confital and the rocky bar near the Punta de Arrecife.

'There are no ships on this side,' he commented.

'No, it's too dangerous for navigation and it's exposed to the prevailing wind. It was on those rocks that we found the unidentified corpse.'

'It isn't likely it came from a ship, then.'

Bernal turned and looked up at towards the dark, beetling snout of El Morro de la Vieja. Below the ridge he could see a high wire fence, with uniformed men patrolling along its perimeter.

'What's up there, Inspector?'

'It used to be a concentration camp during the Civil War. There's a small army camp there to protect the military wireless and radar installations.'

'You mean all the military radio traffic to and from Gran Canaria goes through that station?'

'Yes, that's right. There's also the port radar installation up there, and part of the national defence network.'

'Now that's probably it,' muttered Bernal under his breath, but Lista caught the words. 'That may explain all this strange set-up here.' More loudly he spoke to the local inspector in the rising evening breeze that wafted the smells of the port from far below. 'Let's take a stroll to the cliff-edge before the light goes. You can point out to me exactly where the man's body was found. Then we'll drive down to the morgue and take a look at him and the clothing.'

When they were driven back down the Calle del Faro towards the old port, the darkness fell with sub-tropical suddenness. The wound-down windows of the sleek black Mercedes let in a slipstream of increasingly warm, spicy and contaminated air that felt thick upon the faces of the two detectives from Madrid, unused to the rapid changes of temperature as one moved from high to low ground on the surprisingly varied topography of this island. Bernal supposed that Guedes would never have appreciated the exotic menace of this multiracial city, which tended to keep his Peninsular nerves at a pitch of excitement. Somewhere, he thought, Consuelo was being held against her will; he felt sure she was not dead, or somehow he would have sensed it. He must ring the Civil Guard lieutenant as soon as they reached the Miller Bajo police-station to find out if there was any news.

In Guedes's office, he and Lista examined the clothing and miserable effects of the unidentified corpse, from the worn plimsolls to the waistcoat with the strange pair of holes in the breast-pocket. Bernal gazed at the perforations in some puzzlement: hadn't he seen marks like that very recently?

'This waistcoat must have had a badge of some kind attached to it, Lista, but it must have been quite a large and heavy one.' Bernal racked his memory. 'Don't airport porters and dock-workers wear badges in their lapels?'

'Anyone who works in a place with a system of security checks does, *jefe*. Official drivers, airport employees, bank security personnel and so on.'

'But these are the clothes of a poor person, Lista. The two things don't quite add up, except possibly in the case of a stevedore.' Bernal took a glass and examined the strains and tears in the cloth more closely. 'These perforations remind me of something I saw the other day, in Madrid. But I can't recall what it is. I'm getting old, Lista; my memory's failing.'

'Nonsense, chief. I'm twenty years younger than you and they don't remind me of anything. Look at the wear on the soles of these plimsolls. That's not the regular wear one finds from heel to the ball of the foot. It suggests that the unidentified man used to shuffle rather than walk normally. It's the same on both shoes. How old did the pathologist say he was?'

'He put him at forty-five to fifty.'

A brief inspection of the cadaver in the mortuary nearby told them little more, except that the hollow ocular cavities set deep in the slightly greenish pallor of the face suddenly brought Bernal's recollection flooding back.

'Those perforations in the waistcoat pocket, Lista. They could have been made by the metal clipboard the lottery-ticket sellers wear to carry the daily tickets. He could have been a blind man. That would explain the unusual wear on the soles of the plimsolls. Ask Guedes to check it out with the local Delegación of the ONCE to see if any of their vendors is missing or has failed to turn up for work in the last three days. He could also ask for a clipboard to check against the marks on the clothing.'

When Lista returned, he looked grave. 'There's an urgent message for you, chief. The Civil Guard have found Señora Lozano's blue Renault abandoned at Telde, but there's no sign of her. The lieutenant is waiting for you at the *cuartel* there to accompany you to the scene. He's sent for a finger-prints expert from the Policía Judicial to check the car for prints.'

'Let's go out there at once, Lista. I'd prefer to see it for myself before the locals mess it up.'

As the large Mercedes swept along the Avenida Marítima past the Naval Base, the waves breaking on Las Alcaravaneras beach were luminously pink with the afterglow of the sunset. With no time to admire the twilight view of the Bay, Bernal switched on the rear reading-light to peruse the local forensic lab's report on the water samples taken from the different mains supplies that served Las Palmas and its environs. He passed the analyst's findings to Lista and lit a Kaiser.

'Strange, isn't it? The deceased man is found half-submerged in sea-water, yet he drowned in fresh water, according to the local path lab. I wonder if they've run the tests properly; although they may be used to cases of "blue" and "white" drownings, are they experienced in homicide cases?'

'I shouldn't have thought they'd have more than a handful of murders a year on this island, chief, and then they'd be simple domestic cases or the result of tavern brawls.'

'Exactly, Lista.' Bernal took a sudden decision. 'Get on the radio to Navarro and ask him to contact Madrid. I want Dr Peláez out here, as well as Varga and the deputy technician. I need the top pathologist's opinion on the drowned man, and I want our best technician to check out that abandoned house up at La Isleta. There's far too much débris for the local inspector to manage, and he's got no trained men at his station.'

As Lista was speaking on the radio with Navarro, the Mercedes was just emerging from the short road tunnels by the Punta del Palo when the police driver braked to take the turn-off on to the old road that led due south to Telde. They were now entering a lusher countryside which they could dimly glimpse in the gathering dusk, where there were thick orange-groves and clumps of more exotic fruit-trees bearing avocados, custard-apples, mangoes and loquats.

'Did you know that the best oranges in the world are grown here at Telde, Lista?'

'You've been swotting up on the place, as usual, *jefe*.'

'Well, I must admit to reading a history of Gran Canaria

to while away the time at Barajas and on the plane. There's no such thing as useless information.'

The driver switched on the high beam as they descended the winding road, the only natural light now remaining being a faint afterglow on the high cloud forming on the eastern horizon. Ahead they could see the street-lights of the old town of Telde, which presented a markedly North African outline with its church towers gleaming faintly white and gold like minarets.

'You'd think you were in Ceuta or Tangiers, chief,' commented Lista.

'I've never been in either place, but I'd guess it's more the heady scent of the orange-blossom that gives one the idea.'

The police driver stopped at the Civil Guard post to ask the way before beginning to negotiate the narrow side-streets where he had to crawl in order to stop and look at the nameplates at the corners. At the end of the town to the south-east they found two Civil Guard jeeps parked near a stretch of waste ground. The lieutenant Bernal had got to know at Gando airport came over to greet them.

'We've fingerprinted all the surfaces of the car, Comisario. It's definitely Señora Lozano's. The insurance papers issued by the hire firm were in the glove-compartment.'

'Have you searched the interior and the boot thoroughly?' asked Bernal.

'Yes, Comisario, and there's nothing to help us discover where she was taken. I've questioned all the people living in these houses who happen to be at home, and they claim to have heard and seen nothing, but that's a typical reaction to the Civil Guard in these parts,' he ended somewhat bitterly.

Bernal borrowed a powerful torch from one of the men and swept it over the interior and exterior of Consuelo's car, and then knelt down to look underneath. Finding nothing, he began to move the beam over the waste ground beyond the broken asphalt.

'There are a number of tyre-marks in the dust there,

Lieutenant. Shouldn't we take plaster casts of them? From the track widths they could have been made by a jeep or even a small van.'

The officer looked crestfallen. 'My men made a circular turn there before they spotted the abandoned Renault. The sun was in their eyes.'

Bernal sighed with frustration, but moved further on to the wasteland, stopping again to observe some tracks.

'I can see the most recent marks of the turning circle made by your men, Lieutenant, but here's a semi-circular track that is older, with its edges a bit blurred by the wind. This is a much wider track than the Civil Guard jeep. Have you got a tape-measure?'

It was Lista who produced a metal reel and Bernal compared the widths. 'Half as wide again. It must have been a medium-sized van or truck. The tyre-treads are different, too.'

'We'll make casts of it, Comisario.'

'At once,' Bernal ordered. 'The evening breeze will blur the marks further and we'll be unable to match the tyre-patterns. Look, there are separate tracks for each wheel where the driver turned sharply to regain the roadway. Take the casts there.'

'We'll also need to get a sample of Señora Lozano's fingerprints from the house, Comisario. The one thumbprint on her *carnet de identidad* won't be sufficient to eliminate hers from the other latents we've obtained from her car.'

'I'll telephone her maid to tell her to expect the lab technician,' said Bernal. 'She can show him what the Señora will most recently have touched, such as her dressing-table and the wardrobe doors. I'll warn her not to do any dusting in the meantime.'

In the doorway of one of the mean houses Bernal noticed a small girl gazing at them curiously through a dirty-looking Californian curtain. She was shaking something in her cupped hands.

'*Hola, chiquilla.* Did you see a lady here yesterday getting out of the blue car? A large blonde lady wearing a pretty frock with flowers on it?'

The girl shook her head shyly and made to withdraw. Bernal noticed something blue and shining in the grubby palms of her olive-skinned hands.

'What have you got there, *miniña*? Is it a nice toy?'

She opened her hands fully to reveal a broken transparent plastic container and a small pile of iridescent blue beads.

'Oh, is it broken, then?'

The little girl nodded her head sadly.

'Shall I give you some money to buy a new one?' Bernal had infinite patience with child witnesses, being used to his own sons long ago and his present unruly grandson, and he often found that they repaid it with useful information. 'What is it that you've got?'

The little girl shook the few beads inside the battered plastic container. 'A rattle, but it's broke. I found it there.' She pointed towards Consuelo's Renault.

'By the car? Is that where you found it?' Bernal waved a hundred-peseta note in front of her suddenly mesmerized eyes. 'There. That's to buy a new one. Will you show me just where you found it?'

She approached the car along the last part of the cobbled pavement with great reluctance, but following the proferred banknote as if it were the Holy Grail. From above her tiny head Bernal waved to the uniformed guards to retire out of sight behind the wall of the end house.

'Just show me where you found it, and this is yours to buy a new one or anything else you like. Your mummy will take you to the shop tomorrow.'

Still clutching the broken rattle, the girl reached the corner of the street and pointed to a spot near a storm-drain.

'Will you put it back where and how you first saw it?'

With obvious reluctance the grubby creature squatted in the dusty roadway and placed the plastic container just under the edge of the ledge of the drain and carefully piled the beads on it. Shining his torch into the opening Bernal spotted two more blue beads winking in the accumulated dirt. There were some heavy tyre-marks in the gutter.

'And did you see the lady here? The lady who came in that blue car? A very stout lady, with a flowery skirt? Perhaps there were men with her?'

The child shook her head uncertainly, and suddenly snatching the note from Bernal's hand, she ran back to her house and disappeared behind the curtain of plastic strips.

'Shall I go after her?' asked Lista, coming up to Bernal's side.

'No, leave her be. She's too young to tell us much and if you get the mother involved there'll be a long rigmarole to get through to no purpose. We must contact Señora Lozano's maid at once to see if her mistress had bought this blue rattle. There's only half its case here and it's a bit battered, but the plastic seem to be new and unchewed. You can see where it's split along the seam in the moulding.' Bernal counted the beads. 'There are six with the rattle and two more in the drain. Now how many would it have contained, I wonder?' He shone the torch on to the half-container to judge its volume. 'Probably seventy or eighty just in this half, but it would only have been half full at best to allow it to make a satisfactory noise.'

'If it was Señora Lozano's, do you think she dropped it deliberately to leave a trail?'

'It could be. It may have broken in the struggle and she shoved it out when her abductors were putting her into another vehicle. See, Lista, here are the heavy tyre-tracks in the gutter. Get on the car radio and ask Control to ring the maid. Here's the number.'

While Lista went back to the Mercedes, Bernal showed his find to the Civil Guard officer.

'Those large rattles are all the rage, Comisario. My baby

daughter has been given one with pink beads that's other-wise identical to it.'

'Do you know where they are sold?'

'I'm not sure. My sister gave it as a present. In one of those specialist baby shops, I expect. They're supposed to be non-toxic and indestructible, but kids always find a way to break them, don't they?'

'If it should prove to belong to Señora Lozano, we'll have to search for more of the beads, on the supposition that she dropped them deliberately to leave a trail, like Ariadne in the maze. How many beads would you say are in the one that your baby daughter has?'

The lieutenant looked speculatively at the plastic con-tainer in Bernal's hand. 'I'd say more than fifty. They're perfectly light, as you can tell. The rattles are pretty large, on purpose for the babies not to be able to put them in their mouths.'

Lista returned from the police car. 'The maid's in quite a state, the girl at Control tells me. She's still hysterical, not having heard from her mistress at all. She says that Señora Lozano came home the day before yesterday—the day she went to see her doctor in the evening—with some items from the baby shop for the crèche, including a large transparent rattle with blue beads in it, which she left on the hall-stand, but it's not there now. She assumes that the Señora must have taken it with her some time yesterday.'

'Now why would she do that?' asked Bernal, more hopeful of being able to track down Consuelo and her abductors. 'She has the baby's crèche ready in a small bedroom; I've seen it myself. Why didn't she leave it there?'

'The wrong colour, I suppose,' suggested the lieutenant brightly. 'Perhaps she was going to change it for a pink one. Maybe the doctor had told her she was going to have a daughter.'

Bernal shut his eyes with sudden grief and longing at this suggestion, and hoped his colleagues couldn't see his reaction in the dark. He swallowed and said: 'Check it out with her doctor, Lista. Her maid should know who he is. In the meantime we'd better get your men organized to make a search for more of these beads, though it won't be easy in the dark.'

'I'm not sure how she would manage to drop more of them if she was taken away in a closed vehicle,' commented the lieutenant.

'But if it was a truck or a van with the windows open, she might try,' said Bernal, 'assuming she wasn't tied hand and foot. The maid said that the wide skirt had a large patch pocket on each side at the front. Perhaps she'd been carrying the rattle in one of the pockets and it broke in the struggle when she was seized. That would mean that the other half of the container and the remaining beads would still be available to her to leave a trail if she could get at them from time to time.'

'If she could do that, Comisario, wouldn't she try to do so when the vehicle in which they were taking her made a turn from one road to another? Why don't we start at the main road that passes through the centre of town and search that thoroughly? There's better street-lighting there, and her abductors are bound to have emerged on to the main road whichever way they went from Telde. Alternatively, if we find nothing there, we can backtrack to this point on the assumption they are holding her in Telde itself.'

'An excellent suggestion, Lieutenant. Let's take all your available men and one driver to help us. We'll need more torches.'

'I'll radio through to the *cuartel* and ask for extra men and a supply of torches. We've got enough beads to show them what they're looking for.'

After dark that evening, Consuelo could see through the gaps in the boarding of her cell the glare of the camp-fires across the volcanic waste, where the cooks seemed to be preparing the evening meal for the mercenaries. She had noticed, after the alarm caused by the seismic rumbling and the appearance of a large steaming crack along at least a third of the width of the *caldera*, that some of the tents had been hastily struck and not put up again. Did this mean they intended to move camp? The idea worried her in the extreme, for, in the earlier confusion, she had managed to pocket a thick kitchen knife when the old woman's back was turned and before Tamarán or one of his henchman locked her in her cell once more. The knife had not been missed, or, if it had, the old woman had kept silent about it.

The problem was now the timing of her escape. She would have to wait for the evening broth and the hunk of *gofio* to be served to her and the dishes removed. Then she'd be given a can of water for the night. Consuelo noticed that the floor of the cavern was still too hot to walk on in bare feet, and she examined her battered white high-heeled shoes ruefully: if only she had been allowed to bring her flat-heeled driving shoes from the car! It was her own vanity that had brought her to this pass; she had wanted to look elegant for Luis (though what normal person would expect to be kidnapped when simply driving to an airport to collect a passenger?)

Thinking of Luis made her wish desperately that he would get a move on in spotting the trail she had left, for she remained confident he would realize the significance of the clues she had dropped. But how long would it take to follow them, especially in the dark? Consuelo guessed that the car had been found by now, so long as it hadn't been hidden by some of Tamarán's fellow conspirators.

The island was comparatively densely populated, although she realized there were plenty of wild areas, especially up in the Cumbres, in the foothills of which she was now confined. Nevertheless, cars, apart from those of passing tourists, were rare in the remoter spots and an abandoned one would attract notice among the local people. It would be easier to conceal one in the city, she reasoned, in

a large car-park or in a lock-up garage. But if the Alcorán
gang, as she had now come to think of these fanatical
terrorists, had been careless, and left her car in the outskirts
of Telde, then the Guardia Civil would surely have discovered it by now after Luis had put out a general alert. But
night had fallen and they hadn't tracked her to this lonely
valley. The trail wouldn't be easy to follow because of the
widely spaced intervals between the places where she had
managed to drop some more of the beads. Oh God, what if
some of them had got lost down drains or been picked up by
children, or even birds? Their iridescence would make them
attractive.

She felt a sudden sharp contraction and lay doubled up on
the bed for a while. Please, please God don't let the child
come early, before I can escape up the hillside to a phone.
Although normally the least religious of persons, Consuelo
prayed vehemently. Soon the pains passed and she risked
getting up to make another reconnaissance through the
boards. The soldiers were queueing up with metal cans that
gleamed in the firelight to receive a dollop of the ill-smelling
rancho and a mug of wine, which seemed to be their twice-
daily ration. She'd have to wait until they settled down to
smoking and gambling. Once the talk was loud and drunken,
and the old woman had cleared away the utensils left by the
officers in the large cavern, Consuelo decided to make the
final effort to free sufficient boards to get her not inconsiderable bulk out into the velvety darkness lit only by the stars,
since the moon had not yet risen.

After ten minutes had gone by, the men across the newly
formed crevasse began to sing and clap to a pop song turned
up on a portable radio, while the officers' conversation
got loud and drunken in the large cavern. The old woman now
came to collect Consuelo's untouched dish of cabbage stew,
and handed her a can of water, slamming the door with
a rough goodnight. Despite her brusqueness in front of
Tamarán, Consuelo had gained the impression that she

was now warmer in her manner than when she had first arrived; a kind of womanly fellow-feeling, perhaps.

Once the officers' talk reached a crescendo, Consuelo decided to make a determined assault on the remaining boards that blocked her only possible means of escape. She touched the shape of the rusty knife she had hidden under the dirty blanket and patted it with satisfaction. How wonderful it would be to get to civilization and have a hot bath!

Superintendent Bernal wished he'd brought an overcoat with him, since the evening had turned chill at Telde, with a stiff breeze blowing up off the sea. He had expected Gran Canaria to be cooler than Madrid in July, but he hadn't calculated that up in these foothills a lightweight suit would be decidedly insufficient. He slapped his arms together as he accompanied Lista along the western pavement of the main street towards the southern end of the town.

Two Civil Guards with walkie-talkies were searching the eastern side of the roadway opposite him, but Bernal reasoned that if the abduction vehicle had turned south towards the airport and Maspalomas once it had reached the main road, then he and Lista were more likely to find on the right-hand side any clues that Consuelo had managed to drop. Bernal had already radioed Paco Navarro to send out Ángel Gallardo and Elena Fernández to reinforce the search-party. They and the Civil Guard lieutenant were proceeding slowly northwards searching on each side of the highway towards Las Palmas.

There was a sudden whistle from across the street. 'Over here, Comisario! We've found another bead in the gutter.'

Greatly cheered by the news, Bernal and Lista crossed the roadway on which there was very little traffic now at nearly 9.0 p.m. when most people were taking their evening meal.

'It's definitely the same as the others, chief,' commented Lista, comparing it with the ones he had already placed in a small plastic bag.

'Now how can it have got to this side of the road?' asked Bernal in puzzlement. 'If the vehicle Señora Lozano was taken away in came out of the side-streets of the town and then turned southwards, the beads should have fallen out on the west side of the road where we've been searching.'

'There's an exit from the side-streets just here, Comisario,' one of the Civil Guards pointed out. 'Although it's no more than an unsurfaced lane, they may have taken this exit rather than the one we came out on.'

'That's possible,' Bernal conceded, 'but it could mean that Señora Lozano was already dropping beads out of her own car window between the airport and here, before the abductors changed vehicles. The Gando road comes in past here, doesn't it?'

'Yes, sir, that's right.'

Lista now intervened. 'If the abductors after capturing her at the airport were bringing her here in the blue Renault, perhaps having bundled her into the back seat of it, or forcing her to drive at gun-point, would she have been able to drop these clues unobserved? Perhaps it was only later, after they changed to the larger vehicle, the truck or whatever it was, that she managed to begin dropping the beads whenever they made an important turn just as at this street corner.'

'If you're right, Lista, that still doesn't tell us whether the vehicle turned left or right at this point, so we'd better not lose time. We should go on searching both sides of the roadway as before until we find another clue or until Ángel and Elena radio to us to say they've found one.' Bernal turned to the two guards before he and Lista re-crossed the road. 'Remember to look out for other likely objects, such as the contents of the Señora's handbag. She may not have had enough of these beads.'

It had suddenly become quiet in the cavern, and Consuelo lay still, holding her breath in her anxiety. Tamarán and his henchmen had gone to a vehicle and started it up. Soon she could hear it begin to ascend the steep curving track that led up to the rim of the *caldera*. From the noise of the engine she judged it to be a high-powered car, perhaps the black Mercedes that had followed her the day before, or was it two days ago? She was losing her grasp of the passage of time, she realized. Perhaps she should have carved the dates on the boards of her prison, but that seemed to be an action of despair. She expected to be out of this dreadful place in short order now. The whine of the low gear the driver of the car had engaged faded away, and she could hear only the drunken singing and quarrelling of the men round the camp-fires some three hundred metres away. She hoped the old woman was asleep, through she couldn't hear her snoring yet.

Clutching the kitchen knife, Consuelo made her way silently to the boarded-up window and began work feverishly to loosen the rough planks. The middle one came away easily, and soon she managed to loosen one end of the one below it. Holding her breath again to listen, Consuelo tugged at it with all her strength and it came free with a sudden jerk, throwing her backwards on to the truckle-bed where she landed with a loud thud.

Now she listened with alarmed intentness: surely the old woman would have heard? Or one of the sentries outside? But no one came. Getting up cautiously, she placed the plank quietly on the floor and took deep gulps of the cold night air that now entered from the wide gap. She risked putting her head out to reconnoître. Apart from the noisy soldiers who were too far away to notice anything, she saw nothing in the darkness. When her eyes got more accustomed to the dense gloom, she spotted the glow of a cigarette some fifteen metres away near the farm truck parked at the start of the track down which they had brought her. A sentry, she thought, she'd have to be very careful. She turned to the next plank and began to work on it with the rusty kitchen knife. She calculated that removing one more plank would be enough to allow even her bulk through the window-frame, but this was too high to reach comfortably.

Consuelo manhandled the truckle-bed as silently as she could towards the window and sat on it to regain her breath and to listen. There was still no sound from the old woman in the main part of the cave. Standing somewhat shakily on the badly made wooden base of the *catre*, she started on the last plank blocking her escape. This proved to be a much tougher proposition, and she swore under her breath as one of the nails jagged her finger. Oh Lord, she would need an anti-tetanus injection when she got to safety, and wouldn't that be harmful to her unborn child? As though answering her, the fœtus gave a hefty kick inside her abdomen and she nearly swooned with pain. Then with sudden determination she forced the nails out of the surrounding frame and the plank came away and fell on top of her, laying her flat on the creaking bed. Her senses swam for a while and she panicked at the noise she had made, but no one came, nobody had noticed. With no little feeling of triumph, Consuelo climbed on the sill and slid her legs into whatever unknown perils lay outside. The frame was narrower than she had realized and she felt the rough wood tear at her voluminous skirt. She couldn't touch the ground with her feet—the drop on the outer side must be greater than on the inner. Now came the problem of squeezing her huge belly through, without doing the baby or herself any harm. Soon she realized that she was stuck, being able neither to get in nor out. She began to sob with frustration, until she was shocked into silence by some-one's hands clutching her legs.

Oh God, she thought, the sentry had noticed her attempt to get away. But the hands helped her to squeeze out, freeing the folds of her skirt from the impeding window-frame. Slowly she was helped down and a smelly hand was placed over her mouth and nose.

'Not that way! They'll see you!' whispered a hoarse voice. 'Come with me.'

Of course the old woman had heard her removing the boards, but had decided, Consuelo quickly reasoned, to assist her so long as it would appear to be an unaided escape. The woman led her behind the farm truck, sliding between it and the rocky outer side of the cavern and away from the two sentries who were seated having a smoke. The woman tapped Consuelo's arm and pointed towards the rock-strewn slope, whispering in her ear a warning not to loosen any stones. Soon they had gained higher ground above the cavern and some twenty metres to the left of the track.

'Now follow this road, but hide if a car comes! *Váyase con Dios*—Go with God.'

In a sudden pang of gratitude, Consuelo kissed the old woman on the cheek before she slipped away into the deeper shadows.

Stopping to catch her breath, Consuelo glanced down anxiously at the two sentries, but they were talking in low voices and looking towards the noisy scene by the camp-fires, where they probably wished to be. She must be very careful not to loosen any pebbles until she was out of their earshot. She looked up at the starry sky and the dark mass of the side of the *caldera*, the height of which dispirited her. Would she ever make it in her condition up that winding track with its hairpin bends? Gradually she edged upwards, the clean coldness of the mountain hurting her lungs.

After about a quarter of an hour, she sat for a while on a rock. The sentries were now far below her to the left, so she judged that she could now walk at a more normal pace. She looked at her watch: 9.12 p.m. Where, oh where, was Luis? Surely they had found some of the clues she had managed to drop?

An hour and a half later, when Consuelo thought she had got about half way up the side of the volcanic crater, she heard a loud whirring from above her head, and suddenly powerful lights began to sweep over the rocky hillside. She crouched in terror under a large boulder. Had they noticed her absence and called the helicopters back to search for her? She could now see the four of them coming in from the east. Like clumsy dragonflies they made for the camp-fires and then settled beside them raising a cloud of dust that momentarily blotted out their navigation lights.

They didn't seem to be searching for her, then; perhaps the troops were being moved out after the seismic activity there during the morning? There were still eight days to go before 'Plan Mencey' was to be put into operation—or was it nine? She realized she had been wrong not to keep count of the days. She also wished she had paid more attention to the details of the routes and times she had seen on the wall-plan in the offices of Alcorán S.A. so as to be able to inform Luis about it. She was sure it was a terrorist operation to coincide with the President's visit to Las Palmas on 18 July, the very day the doctors had given her for the birth of her child! They were clearly planning, with African mercenary help, to take over the islands and make them independent of Spain.

Consuelo hurried on up the stony track, her feet badly cut by the now ruined high-heeled shoes; at least she hadn't broken a heel yet. She was determined to get to a telephone before Tamarán discovered her absence. Was he in one of the helicopters? That's what worried her most. If so, and he went back to the cavern to check up on her, all would be lost. He would send men in the truck to look for her. Throwing caution to the winds, Consuelo began to half run, half walk, as best her bulk would allow.

After the earlier excitement of finding the clue Consuelo Lozano had dropped in the centre of Telde, Bernal and Lista were now rather dispirited an hour and a half later. They were out on the winding country road that led south, without the benefit of the street-lights. Bernal noticed that his electric torch was starting to lose power.

'We'll have to get new batteries and fresh men for the search soon, Lista. And we can't expect these guards to go on indefinitely without a break. You'd better radio through to the lieutenant and see if he can rustle up some *bocatas* and coffee from the Civil Guard post for us, and reliefs for these men, who've been on duty since two p.m.'

'You ought to get some rest yourself, chief,' commented Lista. 'I could send for the car for you to lie down in the back seat for a while.'

'No, it's my duty to go on,' said Bernal wearily, stopping to peer at a folding map with his rapidly dimming torch. 'Look, we can't be far from this junction where a minor road runs westward up into the Cumbres. There's no other turning apparently for about four kilometres until Cuatro Puertas, where the airport road goes off to the south-east.'

'All right, chief, but if we find nothing at this next junction, then I'll call for the car. You must take a rest and have a snack.'

As they proceeded along the hard shoulder, lizards scurried occasionally from under their feet into the scrub, and they were almost deafened by the grating of the cicadas, some of which hopped into the light of their torches. When they breasted a rise in the road and could see a signpost not far ahead, the radios carried by the two Civil Guards on the other side of the road crackled into life.

'The lieutenant is asking if he should send over reliefs for you and the inspector to go in and get some supper, Comisario.'

'Has his party found anything?'

'Nothing, and they've gone a kilometre to the north of the town.'

'Tell him we'll inspect this next junction and then contact him again.'

The small signpost pointed to CALDERA DE LOS MARTELES and Bernal asked one of the guards whether he knew the road.

'It only leads to four small villages and then it's a dead end, Comisario. It runs almost up to Pozo de las Nieves, one of the highest peaks on the island, where there's a television relay transmitter, but there's no connecting road leading to Tejeda. It's very difficult terrain up there.'

'Let's search the road junction carefully,' Bernal instructed them. 'Lista and I will take the entrance to the mountain road, while you two search the main road beyond the turning.'

At first they found nothing. Lista, however, who had gone on ahead of Bernal along the mountain roadside, wandered into the scrub of euphorbias to the right of the narrow carriageway and suddenly gave a triumphant cry.

'Here are some more beads, chief. Three of them.'

Bernal hurried to the spot and they searched the surrounding area.

'Here's another!' said Bernal.

They found five in all, the last one some twenty metres up the mountain road.

'They must have fallen in this direction as the truck or whatever it was swung into the minor road, chief. They obviously took this route up into the hills.'

'If the guards find nothing on the main road just beyond this turning, that will confirm it,' commented Bernal cautiously. He consulted his map again. 'This will greatly simplify our task, Lista. There appears to be no way through for wheeled traffic at the upper end of this mountain road, which runs alongside the Lomo Tegenales for more than twenty kilometres as far as Caldera de los Marteles. We've got them trapped!' he exclaimed with satisfaction. 'We must place a road-block at this point, and examine all the vehicles entering or leaving the area, as well as checking the *carnets* of their occupants.'

'I'll get the Civil Guard to organize it at once, chief.'

'Let it be done discreetly, out of view of the main road. It could be mounted beyond the first curve in the minor road. That way any of the abductors returning to the hideaway will not be put off before turning.'

Lista went to the radio carried by the older of the guards to transmit Bernal's instructions to the lieutenant.

'Tell him to send his men back to the *cuartel* and ask Ángel and Elena to come and pick us up in the official car,' Bernal shouted after him.

When Lista returned, he asked his chief whether he wanted to be driven up the mountain road.

'We'd better leave it until first light, Lista, and see what the road-block produces. I don't want to put too much pressure on them in case they kill Señora Lozano.' He shuddered at the thought.

'But how will we find out where they are hiding out if we don't send the Civil Guard to search?'

'It would be useless in the dark. Find out if they have a helicopter available. If there is someone who knows the terrain very well and could recognize the various dwellings from the lights shown, he might spot something unusual, such as a camp-fire. But it would be a long shot, and would give them warning that we were close on their trail.'

Five minutes later they heard a car approaching from the direction of Telde, one of the first they had seen for more than an hour; most of the vehicles that had passed had been agricultural.

'It's the black Mercedes, chief. This will be Elena and Ángel.'

'Thank heaven,' said Bernal, 'I shan't be sorry to get into the warm.'

He, Lista and the two Civil Guards were much surprised when the Mercedes swept past them with a scream of its tyres as it took the turn into the Marteles road.

'That wasn't them, *jefe*,' gasped Lista. 'There were four uniformed men in it.'

'What kind of uniforms?' asked Bernal.

'Not ones I recognized,' said Lista.

'Nor did I,' commented the older guard.

'Did you get its number?' asked Bernal.

'Only the *matrícula* GC- and the first three numbers: 892–,' replied Lista ruefully.

'What about you two?' Bernal asked the Civil Guard.

''Fraid not, Comisario. Thinking it was the police car, I didn't pay too much attention.'

Consuelo thought she would die from the stitch in her side. She prayed that she was near the end of the track, now that the sky seemed lighter with the stars less cut off by the towering rocky mass of the crater. She had become inured to the lizards, cicadas, beetles and large spiders that brushed against her ankles; these small creatures would normally have alarmed her, especially having heard stories of poisonous ones. She had even shrugged off her fright at some larger animals she had distinctly heard moving stealthily in the undergrowth; could they be wild-cats or mountain goats? She hurried on along the stony trail, glad that no vehicle had approached her, nor had the helicopters shown any sign of taking off again. Perhaps the pilots had joined the mercenaries for an evening meal.

She rounded a large boulder and suddenly found herself on a narrow tarmac road. Thank God! Now it would be mostly downhill towards the sea until she came to a house with a telephone. Forgetting the pain in her side and the extraordinary heaviness in her womb, she strode out with more spring in her terribly aching legs. Soon the *caldera* where she had been imprisoned was lost to her view.

After half an hour she saw a fixed light below her to the south: could it be a farm? Surely there would be a phone there, but she could see no way of getting to it from the road. In the far distance to the south-east she could make out headlights of vehicles passing along the main highway to Maspalomas, and then a jet liner coming in to land at Gando airport. This sight cheered her immensely: civilization was at hand!

The road dipped steeply into a hollow and she was pleased

to see a village sign ahead: LAS BREÑAS. Had she seen that on
the way up? She couldn't recall it; all she remembered was
Valle Los Nueves lower down the mountain road. The bulk
of two or three houses now loomed in the darkness, surrounded by trees and the paler shape of flowering creepers.
The dwellings were all in darkness, and she could no longer
see the light of the supposed farmhouse away to the south.

Consuelo decided to knock boldly on the door of the first
house that had a telephone cable leading to it; she could
glimpse telegraph poles and electricity posts leading up as far
as the village. But a sudden fearful thought struck her: what
if the villagers were in league with the terrorists? In that case
they would certainly inform her captors at once of her visit.
She looked carefully at the corner house that jutted into the
roadway: it appeared to be shuttered and unoccupied. She
passed it with caution, rounding the bend into the village
proper.

And there a very welcome sight lay before her: an unlit
telephone-box. Thank God for the Telefónica! But would it
be working? She recalled with dismay the number of times
she had come across vandalized and unusable public telephones in Madrid. Presumably people were much more
law-abiding in this remote spot. She felt in her handbag for
her purse; it was missing. Of course, her captors had taken
it from her. Did she have any loose change in the bottom
of the bag? She ought to ring her maid who would be
distraught, and then call the Civil Guard. It would save long
explanations to the operator.

Thankfully she discovered in the bottom folds a coin that
felt like a five-duro piece. Panting with relief, Consuelo
entered the box and picked up the receiver. Yes, there was a
dialling tone. It was too dark to read the instructions, but she
placed the coin on the upper slide and dialled the number of
her hired *chalé* at Las Palmas. She listened in satisfaction as it
gave the ringing tone. Then it was answered.

'*Sí. Dígame.*'

'This is Consuelo Lozano, *chiquita*.'

'Oh Santa María and all the blessed saints! Where are you, Señora? I've been so worried about you. What happened to you?'

'Listen carefully, Manolita. I was abducted by a Señor Tamarán and his henchmen from Alcorán S.A., that firm I went to visit in the Calle de Pío XII. Have you got that? I've managed to get free and I'm up in the hills west of Telde. I'm calling from a phone-box in a place called Las Breñas. It's above a village called Valle los Nueves.'

The girl sounded hysterical, and Consuelo ordered her to calm down.

'Did Comisario Bernal give you a number to ring? Yes? Then ring it now and tell him what I've told you. Now repeat it to me exactly as I've said it. Then I'll dial 091 to get the Civil Guard and the Police. Ring the Superintendent at once, do you hear?'

Consuelo put down the receiver and leant in considerable pain against the side of the kiosk, pressing her feverish face on to the coolness of the glass. She prayed she wasn't going to give birth unaided in this lonely spot where the inhabitants appeared to be asleep or dead. She made an effort to pick up the receiver once more, and dialled the emergency number. A crisp masculine voice asked her what the emergency was.

'I'm Consuelo Lozano who's been kidnapped. I'm in a phone-box at Las Breñas not far from Telde. Please send an ambulance to fetch me. I'm about to give birth; I'm near my time. Please inform Comisario Bernal at the Policía Judicial that there is a conspiracy of terrorists called the Mencey Plan who are plotting a *coup d'état* here in the Canaries on the eighteenth of July. Please tell him without delay.' Consuelo felt a sudden tearing in her groin and a hot stickiness ran down between her legs. Oh God, had her waters broken because of all the effort she had expended on her escape? More fluid dripped on to her shoes and she slumped on to the floor of the booth just as the headlights of a car being driven furiously up the road picked her out. It squealed to a stop and four uniformed men got out.

At least, thought Consuelo, now only semi-conscious, these soldiers will take me to a hospital for me to have my child. She struggled to keep her tired eyes open against the glare of the car's headlights, then cringed in terror as she recognized the haughty features of Señor Tamarán.

Bernal, Lista and the two Civil Guards were still recovering from their surprise at the black Mercedes passing them at high speed when another large car came into sight on the road leading from Telde. It pulled up at the junction and Ángel and Elena Fernández got out.

'Shall we go after them, chief?' asked Ángel eagerly. 'We spotted them when they passed us at a great lick coming in from Las Palmas. Our driver took their registration number and radioed it through to Traffic Control. It was doing over a hundred and twenty kilometres an hour through the northern outskirts of Telde.'

'I don't want them followed for the moment, Ángel, not to put too much pressure on them in case they kill Señora Lozano. It certainly looks as though we've got them boxed in up there. There's no other road out.' Bernal turned to the driver of the police Mercedes. 'Radio in to your control and ask them to find out who owns that black car. There were four uniformed men in it.'

'We could follow them up with caution, chief, to see where their hide-out is,' Ángel suggested.

'Now hold your horses,' said Bernal firmly. 'We need reinforcements first and it will be very difficult, if not impossible, to locate them and mount a raid in the dark. It's very mountainous terrain.'

The Civil Guard jeep now arrived with the lieutenant and three men.

'We can mount the road-block now, Comisario.'

'Things have developed a bit, Lieutenant. The abductors

will certainly have seen us searching here as they passed a couple of minutes ago. We'll have to change our plans.' Bernal spread out his folding map on the bonnet of the police Mercedes and shone his torch on it. 'Now where do you think they would hide out? In one of the villages?'

The officer looked at the map and shook his head. 'Unless they were well paid, the locals would talk. We don't know what these criminals are up to, of course, but if it's smuggling the local people would keep quiet about it. If it's political they might also turn a blind eye.'

'Especially if it's an independence movement, eh?' commented Bernal. 'If not in one of the villages, where?'

'We've had kidnappings of industrialists and businessmen for a ransom of a so-called "political tax". They've some-times used one of the volcanic craters to hide out in, and there's one up this road called the Caldera de los Marteles. You could hide an army in that with all the caverns in its sides.'

'Show me exactly where it is on the map. How would you get down to it?'

'The edges are very steep and there's no motorable road that I know of. Perhaps there's a track between Valle los Nueves and Las Breñas.'

'I hope you're wrong and that they don't actually have an army down there, Lieutenant. I think we should ask for an immediate helicopter reconnaissance to see if anything can be spotted, and major land reinforcements. Our plan will be to move with one group rapidly up the valley, stopping anyone on the move, and with a follow-up group to search every dwelling and side-track.'

The night telephonist at the main Teléfonos building in the Calle de León y Castillo sat back in amazement at Consuelo Lozano's emergency call as the line went dead.

'A real nut-case I've got tonight,' he commented to his companion. 'A woman called Lozano who says she's been

kidnapped and is having a baby in one of our boxes outside
Telde. She even claims that a group of terrorists is planning
to take over the islands on the eighteenth.'

'You'd better report it to the Guardia Civil and the Policía
Nacional just the same. Where exactly was she phoning
from?'

'Somewhere called Las Breñas. I think it's a hoax. That'll
make it the seventh this week. I haven't read in the papers
anything about a woman being kidnapped, have you?'

'Perhaps the police don't know about it yet. You'd better
get on to them pretty quick, because that automatic record-
ing device on the emergency lines will show the time the call
was received. There'll be trouble if you don't report it and it
turns out to be true.'

The younger operator was looking up an internal
company directory. 'Here's the number of that box at Las
Breñas. I'll call back to see if she's still there, since she rang
off.'

He dialled the number and waited for the ringing tone, but
the line gave the number unobtainable sound. 'That's odd.
The line's gone dead up there.'

'Ring the police straightaway,' urged his companion. 'She
might have been telling the truth.'

Bernal's plan to have a two-tier, slowly tightening cordon
was put into operation. Two Civil Guard jeeps, with Ángel
riding in one of them, advanced steadily up the mountain
road, while three more vehicles containing additional uniformed men with Lista in charge, went in the rear, investigating each remote dwelling as they came to it, and all the farm
tracks leading off the metalled road.

In the meantime Bernal was driven back with the lieutenant and Elena in the police Mercedes to the *cuartel* at Telde,
where he rang Paco Navarro at the Gobierno Civil in Las
Palmas in order to update his information and ask him to act
as liaison officer with the Policía Nacional.

No sooner had Bernal and Elena begun to drink some hot coffee than a distraught call from Consuelo's maid was put through to Bernal.

'The Señora's alive and well, Superintendent. She's talked to me on the phone just now,' she said in a gabble of almost breathless excitement.

Trying to calm her down, Bernal asked her to repeat exactly what had been said in the phone call, while his heart sang for joy with the news. 'Did she say who the men were who abducted her?'

'Tamarán, that's who the wicked fellow is. The one she went to see in the Calle de Pío XII the other day. And she told me to be sure to tell you about what they are planning for the eighteenth of July.'

Bernal discovered, however, that it had never become clear exactly what was being planned. 'Did she say how she was?'

'No, but she sounded very weary.'

'We must thank God that she is alive. I'll send men to pick her up at once.'

The lieutenant came in with some more news. 'The helicopter has taken off from Gando. I've sent one of our pilots who was born at Valle los Nueves and therefore knows the whole area well. He warns us about the warren of caves in the sides of the *caldera*, which the aborigines once used as a refuge and as a place to keep their embalmed ancestors in.'

'Radio through to your men and to Inspector Gallardo, and tell them to go straight to the public phone-box at Las Breñas. Señora Lozano has just phoned her maid from there.'

'That's wonderful news. She must have escaped. So we can go in without worry now.'

The phone rang and Navarro came on the line. 'The Policía Nacional has just received an emergency call timed at 11.07 p.m. transmitted from the Telefónica, chief. It was from Señora Lozano asking for police assistance and an ambulance to go to Las Breñas near Telde.'

'An ambulance?' echoed Bernal suddenly disquieted. 'Did they say what her injuries are?'

'No, chief, but they've sent out a medical team from the Policlínica and the Civil Guard has also been notified.'

'You'd better inform the police that in conjunction with the Civil Guard I've mounted a double moving cordon up the valley towards the place where Señora Lozano is. I'll warn them to expect the ambulance.'

Bernal now radioed through to Ángel Gallardo. 'She's escaped, Ángel, and has just rung from the public phone-box at Las Breñas, which is the last village at the head of the valley. An ambulance is on its way from Las Palmas.'

'We'll go there directly, chief. We've just seen the Civil Guard helicopter pass us. It should report in soon.'

Just before midnight a message was relayed from the pilot of the reconnaissance helicopter to the Civil Guard post at Telde: *Lights spotted in the Caldera de los Marteles, probably from camp-fires. Going in to investigate.*

'Tell him to proceed with caution,' Bernal warned the lieutenant. 'There's no need for him to take unnecessary risks. All we want is some idea of their strength.'

Meanwhile Ángel Gallardo with the first Civil Guard detachment had driven at high speed up the mountain road past the first three villages without seeing any sign of the terrorists. Ahead of him Ángel could see the village-sign for Las Breñas, and pulling out his service pistol he told the driver of the jeep to slow down. They entered the shuttered village where Ángel could see a telephone-box at the upper end of the small main street.

'Pull up in front of the phone booth,' he ordered, 'and keep your headlights trained on it.'

He got out and made for the shadows under the nearby building. The guards covered him with their rifles. He could see no trace of Señora Lozano in or near the phone-box, and approached it with great caution, listening for any sound. Pulling open the glass door, he shone his torch inside. The receiver cable had been pulled out and the handset lay on the floor in a thick pool of blood and what appeared to be a scattering of yellowish viscous liquid.

Ángel ran back to the jeep and picked up the radio microphone: 'Put me through to Telde, to Superintendent Bernal.' He waited, wondering how his chief would take the news; he seemed to have a close relationship with the missing Señora, who had invited him to dine with her and who had promised to meet him at the airport. Ángel speculated on whether they had been having an affair: considering Bernal's old battle-axe of a wife who had been short with Ángel on the telephone on a number of occasions, he wouldn't be at all surprised.

The radio crackled and Bernal's voice came on.

'I'm at the phone-booth at Las Breñas, *jefe*. There's no sign of Señora Lozano. The receiver has been torn out of the wall and there's a pool of blood on the floor, with a trail of blood-spots leading out on to the roadway.' Ángel thought he wouldn't mention the more gruesome evidence. 'It looks as if she was lifted into a vehicle and driven away. Shall we pursue?'

There was a grim silence, then Bernal said in a choked voice: 'Proceed with caution up the road beyond the village. The helicopter pilot has reported activity in the volcanic crater below you to the north, although you probably can't see down there yet, judging by the map contours. Remember they may have superior forces and fire-power. Don't go down into the *caldera* until we can send reinforcements, but stop any vehicle trying to escape along the road. Shoot at the tyres if necessary.'

Ángel gave the instructions to the Civil Guard sergeant, who ordered his men back into the two jeeps. One man in each jeep had a sub-machine-gun at the ready as they drove purposefully out of Las Breñas.

*

Paco Navarro rang Bernal from Las Palmas. 'I've just got word from Gando airport, chief. Dr Peláez the pathologist has just arrived on the last flight from Madrid, together with Varga and his assistant technician.'

'Have you booked them into a hotel?'

'Yes, chief. Peláez will be with us in the Don Juan, and Varga and his man will be with Ángel in the Tigaday. I've sent a car to meet them. Have you any instructions for them?'

'Ask Peláez to do a second autopsy on the drowned man found at Las Canteras beach, and tell Varga I want him to liaise with Inspector Guedes at Miller Bajo station to examine the abandoned house up at La Isleta. It's too late for them to start tonight. I suggest they begin first thing in the morning.'

'When are you coming in, *jefe*?'

'When I get definite news about Señora Lozano. Ángel's on her track at Las Breñas, but she's disappeared from the phone-box, and there's a pool of blood there. She must be still alive or they'd have dumped her corpse. I reckon they caught her phoning to us; they tore out the receiver.'

'Chief, the details of that black Mercedes are just coming in. The *matrícula* was issued to Alcorán S.A. with the address in Pío XII, but this year's municipal tax was paid by a José Manuel Tomás, with an address in the town of Arucas, west of Las Palmas.'

'That's very valuable information, Paco. Ask the Policía Nacional to seek confirmation from their local people at Arucas and to put a discreet watch on that address. But they mustn't go in yet.'

Bernal now consulted a wall-map with the Civil Guard lieutenant. 'Are you sure there's no route out of that *caldera* that we haven't covered, Lieutenant?'

'For motor vehicles there's only the one approach and it's very rough and steep. More a job for a vehicle with four-wheel independent suspension rather than a conventional car. The other tracks are only negotiable on mule-back or on foot. Remember they still use pack animals up there.'

Bernal was still worried. 'It seems to me they must have got a way to escape that we haven't thought of. Otherwise they would be trapped in that crater, and they haven't tried to make a break for it down the mountain road. Yet they are bound to have seen your men and us searching at the lower road junction and they'll guess Señora Lozano got a message through, even if they haven't beaten it out of her by now. She may be badly injured. Now why would they still be holding her if they are sure she's informed on them? I don't see the point of it.'

'One possibility is that she found out a lot more about their plans which they may have interrupted her telling us of, Comisario.'

'Another is that they want to hold her as a hostage in case they have to negotiate with us,' concluded Bernal grimly.

When the two jeeps reached the edge of the *caldera*, Ángel and the sergeant could see smoke rising in the light of fires far below them. The Civil Guard helicopter had made a pass to the north-west and was now re-crossing the crater, going in quite low, Ángel observed. The sergeant handed him a pair of night glasses, and he trained them on the camp-fires.

'They seem to be dowsing them, Sergeant. There are a lot of uniformed men, perhaps more than thirty.' Ángel raked the scene with the infra-red prismatics. 'There's a truck parked at the side of the cliff-face, as well as the black Mercedes. Now what are those machines beyond the fires?'

Just then the noise of gun-fire boomed across the crater.

'My God, they're firing at our helicopter!' exclaimed the sergeant.

They watched in horror as the large Sikorski machine tipped drunkenly and then began to regain height, moving rapidly towards their vantage-point.

'Those machines are brown-painted helicopters!' shouted

Ángel. 'I can see the uniformed men getting on board.'

He ran back to the radio in the jeep. Now the Civil Guard helicopter was coming round towards them, its rotors sounding as though they were missing a beat.

'I think he's been hit,' exclaimed the sergeant, signalling in Morse with a green filter over the glass of the powerful lantern he carried. 'I'll let him know we're here.'

Ángel spoke rapidly to Bernal. 'The terrorists have got four helicopters down there at least. The Civil Guard machine has come under fire and it looks as though it's been hit, but it's still in the air.'

'I knew it, Ángel! I figured they must have another means of escape. Stand by while I consult the lieutenant and the airforce base at Gando.'

Ángel and the Civil Guards watched as the green-painted helicopter came in close to the flashing green signalling lamp and then landed on the roadway. The sergeant ran up to open the pilot's canopy.

'Are you OK?'

'They fired at me with small-arms and then with a bazooka, it seemed like. They've hit the fuel tank, I think.' He switched off the engines and climbed down to inspect his machine. 'Yeah, the tank is holed,' he said ruefully. 'Christ, look at those bullet holes!'

'You're lucky they didn't blow you up,' said Ángel.

The lieutenant looked at Bernal gravely after they heard the news of the attack on the helicopter.

'This is going to be a big op, Superintendent. These are no ordinary brigands. They've got more fire-power than just small-arms. The strange uniforms, the bazooka and the four helicopters suggest a large-sized incursion or uprising.'

'We should warn the military governor at once for him to call a full-scale alert,' said Bernal. 'We must have those helicopters tracked by radar. There must be equipment at Gando.'

'It's a bit primitive, I think, Superintendent, especially over land. There's better cover of the maritime approaches for civil and military aircraft which always come in off the sea to avoid the Cumbres.'

'They must do their best. We need to know exactly where they plan to go.'

Ángel and the Civil Guards watched in frustration as the fires were damped down in the crater and the four helicopters started up, their navigation lights flashing green and red. Ángel trained the night binoculars on them.

'We must note the direction they take,' he commented to the sergeant.

When the machines were almost level with the edge of the crater, their navigation lights were suddenly switched off.

'Blast them!' Ángel swore.

'They're taking a hell of a risk of colliding,' commented the Civil Guard pilot. 'If only I could have tracked them.' He kicked the undercarriage of his useless machine in anger.

'The terrain is bad here, isn't it?' said Ángel. 'What route would you take if you were piloting one of them? Show me on the map.'

'I would certainly avoid the peaks of the Pozo de las Nieves and the Roque Nublo, especially in the dark without lights on. We don't know if they have radar on board, of course. If they have, they'd be able to follow the orology, always keeping fifty or sixty metres from possible ground proximity. But there are nasty down-draughts in those peaks. I'd keep a better safety margin than that.'

They stopped talking to listen to the fading noise of the rotor blades.

'They've gone off to the north-west,' said the sergeant, 'so they're keeping away from the high Cumbres.'

'As I thought,' said the pilot, indicating the possible escape route on the map. 'They wouldn't risk going east towards the airport and the military air base. Now they're over a relatively unpopulated area, and once they're north of the Roque Nublo they could make off in any direction.'

'Your lieutenant should have a general alert put out to all Civil Guard units in the island,' said Ángel, picking up the radio handset. 'All the patrols can be told to listen for helicopters without navigation lights showing. At least they can't muffle the noise of the rotors.'

Bernal was fuming with impatience as he overheard the lieutenant's phone call to the airport. 'They've switched off the radar equipment for the night?' he repeated with incredulity.

'After the last civil flight came in. They say they always turn it off until six a.m. It will take some time to switch it back on, apparently, and to get an operator back.'

'It's really beyond belief!' exclaimed Bernal. 'What about the military protection of the island?'

'Oh, they say that system is working at the airforce base, but it will only pick up the four helicopters if they cross the coast in any direction.'

'Tell the airforce personnel to keep a sharp lookout, and I suggest you follow Inspector Gallardo's advice and ask all your patrols to listen for them.'

'Shouldn't we tell your inspector and my men to go down into the crater and make a search? It could be that her abductors have left Señora Lozano tied up there.'

'Yes, but they must be cautious. These terrorists could have left booby-traps.'

Inspectora Elena Fernández now asked her Superintendent whether she shouldn't go up to the Caldera de Los Marteles in case Señora Lozano were found and needed a woman's help. 'I took a course in midwifery when I was at the Escuela de Policía, you know, chief.'

'The ambulance sent from Las Palmas should be up at Las Breñas by now, Elena. The attendants ought to be able to manage.'

*

When the two Civil Guards reached the foot of the rough track leading down to the crater, the sergeant rigged a spotlight to the outer edge of the door and moved it slowly across the abandoned camp site. The fires were still smoking, and one tent was still standing, which had been abandoned in the hurried departure. Ángel examined the farm truck with care, but found nothing of interest. He then approached the black Mercedes parked near the entrance to a cavern, which had boarding broken open on one side.

'That looks like the place Señora Lozano escaped from, Sergeant,' he shouted.

'Be careful, Inspector, there's a deep crevasse opened up here, by volcanic activity, it looks like. It's deep and still steaming with heat from the lava flow.'

Ángel shone his torch over the leather-covered seats of the limousine and saw a lot of fresh bloodstains on the rear seat, as well as a pool of a yellowish viscous substance streaked with blood on the carpet. Could the Señora have started to give birth in the car? If so, where was the child? Taken away with the mother, most probably.

'Señor Lozano was definitely brought here in this car,' he called to the sergeant. 'Let's search the cavern.'

A thorough search revealed the primitive kitchen and sleeping quarters, and the cell with a truckle-bed under the window that had once been boarded up. But there was no sign of any life at all.

Bernal was extremely upset by the report he received from Ángel. 'They've taken her as a hostage, as I suspected,' he said to the lieutenant. 'And she was on the point of giving birth, if she didn't actually go into labour in the car. What sort of animals are these people? If they don't kill her deliberately, she might still die from lack of medical attention.'

The lieutenant thought Bernal was looking grey. 'Why

don't you get some rest, Comisario? We'll make up a bed for
you here if you wish.'

'Very well, but you need some rest too. Elena, you'd better
be driven back to your hotel so that you can be fresh first
thing tomorrow morning to assist Paco Navarro at the
Gobierno Civil. I've a feeling this business is going to take a
few days yet, but we must be on top of them before the
President sets foot on this island.' Bernal turned back to the
Civil Guard officer. 'Be sure to tell your men to wake me if
there's any news during the night. Especially if they find out
where those helicopters have landed. We can't conduct a
detailed examination of the camp-site in the *caldera* until first
light. I suggest you call your men in once you've sent reliefs
to stay on guard.'

Bernal slept little on the camp-bed provided for him in the
officers' quarters at the Guardia Civil post at Telde, partly
because of having to sleep in his clothes in unfamiliar
surroundings, disturbed from time to time by the noise of a
vehicle passing outside the window, but mainly through his
desperate worry over the safety of Consuelo and their child.
Had Ángel told him about everything he had seen in the
abandoned Mercedes and at the hide-out at Los Marteles?
Or, knowing that Consuelo was an intimate friend of his, had
he suppressed some of the gory details? Bernal determined to
go up there to see for himself as soon as dawn came. Then
he would have to go to Arucas to examine the mysterious
Señor Tomás's residence, and later, perhaps at noon, hold a
council of war with his team.

He decided he must also contact Subcomisario Zurdo, his
counterpart at Santa Cruz de Tenerife, to see if his group had
spotted any similar conspiracy in his area, especially since
the President was due there in a few days' time; for a
conspiracy he was now sure it was, judging by the number of
uniformed men involved, and the sophisticated equipment
they clearly possessed. He must seek a meeting also with the

Military Governor as soon as possible, to seek his views on the likely origin of these men. He wondered about the transfer of money, which Consuelo had obviously spotted, on a regular monthly basis from Algiers; that suggested a link-up with Saharan nationalists who in turn were aiding the more home-grown variety.

Bernal sat up on the rickety bed, which was much too small for a man of his weight, and opened a new packet of Kaisers. He tried to work out what the Mencey Plan, which had been mentioned by Consuelo in her emergency phone call, might really involve. Wasn't the very name *Mencey* familiar to him? He'd already seen it in quite common commercial use in Las Palmas; but wasn't it the aboriginal name for some kind of leader? He wished he hadn't left his history of the island by the side of his bed in the hotel.

Bernal woke with a start and looked at his watch with bleary eyes: 7.10 a.m. The heavy scent of orange-blossom borne in through the window of his temporary accommodation at the Telde *cuartel* made him feel slightly sick. No one had disturbed him during the night, which must mean that there was no news, either good or bad, about Consuelo, nor any definite word of the terrorists' new hide-out. Why had they moved from the Caldera de los Marteles? Simply because of Consuelo's escape and subsequent phone call to the authorities? Or had there been some other reason? Ángel had mentioned some localized seismic activity in the crater, which surprised Bernal. Although the Canaries Archipelago was still volcanically active in places, such as Fuerteventura, Tenerife and La Palma, he hadn't read or heard of any in Grand Canary in modern times. But such an event might have been sufficient for Tamarán and his gang to change camp, and their preparations for departure might well have given Consuelo the opportunity to break out. Now, of course, she would be more closely guarded than ever, if she was still alive. He winced and shut his eyes again. Why, oh why, had she decided to meddle in the financial affairs of Alcorán S.A.? She would say it was her job, but he knew that she was inquisitive and persistent by nature. Perhaps these qualities in her had been enhanced by her long relationship with him.

There was a knock on the door and a Civil Guard entered with a bowl of hot water and a towel. 'For you to shave, Comisario. There's a safety razor in the cupboard. Coffee's ready when you want it.'

'Has there been any news during the night?'

'Three reports came in about the helicopters passing over the west of the island, Comisario, but there's no definite news of where they landed. The lieutenant will put you in the picture shortly.'

Bernal found that officer looking as fresh as though he hadn't been on duty for more than thirty-six hours.

'Come and look at this large-scale map, Superintendent. Our patrols reported the noise of helicopters at twelve-fifty a.m. near Artenara, and then just after one near San Nicolás, which is in a remote area to the south-west. The last report came in at one twenty-three from Mogan, where the sergeant-in-charge heard helicopters pass overhead making towards the north-east. There's been nothing since then.'

'And were there any radar contacts?'

The lieutenant looked at him ruefully. 'None, sir.'

'That probably means they haven't left the island, if the sets were working properly.' Bernal marked the sightings on the large relief map. 'It seemed that they made a circuit of almost two hundred and eighty degrees to avoid the Cumbres in the centre of the island. Now north-east of Mogan there are only reservoirs and pinewoods, aren't there?'

'That's right, Superintendent, and no motorable roads. But there are tracks that a jeep could follow.'

'Nevertheless, they must have got an alternative camp which is accessible by metalled road, or they wouldn't be able to bring their troops into action. That means they must be within easy reach of the main southern highway from Mogan to Maspalomas, or somewhere near San Agustín.'

'I've already got my superiors' permission to order a search of the entire south and south-east areas, Superintendent. They'll be starting about now.'

'Don't you think the army ought to be called in to assist?'

The lieutenant looked unhappy at this suggestion that the Benemérita, as the Guardia Civil was honorifically entitled, would not be able to cope. 'My superior officers have called out all our men, Superintendent, and they will know the ground better than the *legionarios*. We've also asked for the loan of a helicopter from the Fuerza Aérea.'

'Very well, Lieutenant. As soon as my inspectors get here I propose to examine the crater at Los Marteles. Later I'll make a trip to Arucas to investigate the owner of that black Mercedes that nearly ran us down last night.'

When Bernal was finishing his coffee and hunk of toast, a police car arrived from Las Palmas bringing Juan Lista and Ángel Gallardo.

'Navarro is organizing everything for Dr Peláez to do the second autopsy on the drowned man, chief,' said Lista, 'and Varga has set out with Inspector Guedes for La Isleta to do a detailed forensic of the empty hovel where the woman was found.'

'He's arranging a conference of all of us at noon, is he?'

'He suggests twelve-thirty, chief, to give you more time to get to Arucas and back.'

They drove up the mountain road from Telde in the grey morning light, sparing hardly a glance for the ever more parched and desolate landscape, where occasional large bulks of dirty polythene covers protected tomato plants from the fierce north-easterly winds. When they got to Las Breñas, Bernal ordered the driver to stop for Ángel to show him the telephone-box. The village seemed curiously deserted, and the pair of Civil Guards left on duty there by the lieutenant saluted the Superintendent as he showed them his credentials. Bernal looked grimly at the bloodstains and the rest of the physical evidence, then returned to the car.

'We'll go down into the crater now.'

One of the Civil Guards came over to talk to the police driver. 'You'd better not take this Mercedes down the rough track. We have a Land-Rover here and we can take the Superintendent and the inspectors.'

Bernal sat hunched uncomfortably in the rear seat of the Land-Rover and held on tight as the ride became bumpy on the steep track. He gazed down at the drop with horror: it was almost unimaginable that Consuelo had succeeded in making that difficult climb in her condition and in the dark. He was convinced she had done herself real injury, as the physical signs she had left in the phone-box surely indicated.

At the bottom of the incline they could see another Civil Guard vehicle and two uniformed men, who saluted the police officers as they alighted.

'Any trouble during the night?' asked Bernal.

'No, sir, none at all, but the lava is still steaming in that deep crack. This old volcano's showing signs of activity. The ground is quite hot to the touch in places.'

The sun came out as the policemen approached the cavern, which they briefly inspected.

'I suggest you go over this hide-out carefully, Lista,' Bernal said, 'in case they've left something important.'

Ángel then accompanied his chief to the abandoned tent, which they found still contained two bed-rolls.

'Undo those and see if you can find anything, Ángel.'

Bernal made his way to the burned-out camp-fires and examined the litter of discarded food, which seemed to have consisted mainly of lamb stew, and then poked at the piles of empty wine-bottles and cans of La Tropical beer and Coca-Cola.

Ángel emerged from the tent carrying a small book and a bundle.

'It's in Arabic characters, chief. I think it's copy of the Kuran.'

'Anything else?'

'Only these.' He showed Bernal a well-thumbed pack of Spanish playing-cards and a grubby bundle of softly pornographic photographs of an Arab dancing-girl in various states of discreet abandon.

'A bit old-fashioned, aren't they?' commented Bernal. 'They look as though they were taken in Tangier during our occupation of it. Let's see what else there is.'

They approached the edge of lightly smoking lava in the crevasse with caution.

'This must have caused them unexpected headaches, Ángel. It extends for four or five hundred metres across the crater floor.'

Ángel walked along the edge of the volcanic crack peering into its depths.

'In places it's only a metre or so deep, chief, but in others I can't see the bottom.'

'Be careful you don't fall in.'

At the end of the crevasse near the cavern entrance Ángel gave a sudden shout. 'There's something down here, chief.' He knelt on the steaming edge. 'It's a body, I'm afraid.'

Bernal stumbled and nearly fell. 'Is it a woman or a man?'

'A woman, sir.' Ángel became suddenly solicitous. 'Look, chief, you go and sit in the Land-Rover while Lista and I handle this.'

Bernal gulped for air, clutching at his heart. 'I'll go and radio in to Navarro. We'll need to get Peláez out here, and the judge of instruction for this *partido judicial*. The Civil Guard will have to bring a special hoist to get her up from there. It's too dangerous for anyone to go down except on a rope.'

After giving orders to Navarro on the Civil Guards' radio, Bernal sat smoking with his eyes shut in the back of the

vehicle. He had never thought of himself as a vengeful
person, but now he felt murderous towards the perpetrators
of such a foul crime. Judicial garrotting would be too good for
them; he would cheerfully disembowel them with his own
hands.

Lista and Ángel Gallardo in the meantime had carried
some of the boards from the cavern and slung them across a
narrower section of the crevasse as near as possible to where
the corpse lay.

'I'm worried about the chief, Juan,' Ángel confided to
Lista. 'I think Señora Lozano was an intimate friend of his,
and he's very cut up about it. Shouldn't we try to persuade
him to go back to the office at Las Palmas? Or go to Arucas to
look at the Tomás fellow's house? Anything to get him away
from here.'

'You won't shift him, Ángel, not until he's seen what he
has to see.' Lista looked down into the steaming cavity. 'How
far down would you say she is?'

'A couple of metres at least. We'll need to erect a hoist over
these planks.'

Almost an hour later a jeep brought the judge of instruction from Telde, accompanied by the Civil Guard lieutenant
and a police surgeon. It was followed by a larger vehicle
bringing special equipment. The Civil Guard team rigged up
a hoist and the judge gave permission for the body to be
raised. Bernal stood with him on the edge of the crevasse,
looking so pale that he might fall down, thought Lista. They
all looked round as the tyres of a large car could be heard
coming down the latter part of the track.

'It's Dr Peláez, our chief pathologist from Madrid,' mur-
mured Bernal to the judge. 'Have you any objection to his
participating in the autopsy?'

'None at all, Comisario. Who do you think has done this
thing?'

'We're dealing with a dangerous and ruthless gang, Judge,
who will stop at nothing to gain their ends. I think they are

independientistas, who are relying on some military aid from the Western Sahara to try and obtain full autonomy for the Canary Isles. Let's hope they don't end up making them a colony of some African state.'

The judge was obviously shocked to hear this. 'Of course we've had á series of independence movements,' he said, 'but they've all fizzled out in time. These young chaps nowadays, influenced by Marxist ideas and helped by foreign money, dream of breaking free of Madrid. It's true that few of us love the Peninsula, indeed most of us have never been there —we've got closer links with the Caribbean—yet it would be disastrous to exchange the devil we know for some African overlord. Those Saharans are only in it for what they can get.'

Peláez emerged from the large police Mercedes, the suspension of which was still rocking from the hair-raising descent, and came towards them with the thick pebble lenses of his spectacles shining with eagerness and joy. He shook hands with them all and then addressed Bernal.

'I've taken a look at the drowned man. A very interesting case. There's no doubt he drowned in fresh water, although he was found in shallow sea-water. He'd had a crack on the head shortly before death. Very fascinating cases you always bring me to. Well worth the trip out.'

'How do you explain what happened to him, then?' asked Bernal.

'Oh, it must be homicide, all right. I found traces of ferrous oxide in the bronchiæ and a faint smell of kerosene in the lung tissue. I suggest you look for some kind of iron tank with stagnant tapwater in it.'

'I think I know just where it is, Peláez. Thank you for giving me the confirmation I needed.'

They both turned to watch as a Civil Guard was lowered on a stout rope into the steaming volcanic crevasse; soon he disappeared from view.

'Is it a woman they're bringing up?' Peláez asked.

'That's right,' Bernal managed to utter in a choked voice. 'Ángel spotted her body soon after we got here.'

When the guard had attached another rope round the waist of the corpse, he was hauled back up, then the cadaver was slowly raised. As it came to the edge, Bernal blenched and turned away to retch. Peláez caught him by the arm and led him to the car.

'You know very well you've never had the stomach for this sort of thing, Luis. Now sit in there and take a sip of brandy from this flask.'

'No, no. I'll be all right.'

A sudden shout from Ángel made them turn their heads. 'I don't think it can be Señora Lozano, chief. This woman is short, swarthy-complexioned, with black hair going grey. She's wearing a ragged black dress. I don't think she fits the description at all.'

Bernal stumbled hastily back to the scene. 'You're right, Ángel. Thank God it's not Consuelo Lozano,' he gasped. 'They must be still holding her as hostage. Now who can this poor soul be?'

The body was laid on a stretcher for Dr Peláez and the police surgeon to examine.

'The time of death will be very difficult to assess, Luis,' called out Peláez. 'She's damned nearly been cooked by the volcanic lava.'

'But was she killed during the past twenty-four hours, say?'

Peláez conferred with the police surgeon as they looked at the thermometers they had inserted into the body.

'A shorter time than that. Ten to twelve hours, probably.'

Bernal and the other officers looked at the poor clothing and the wedding-ring worn thin on the annular finger of the right hand.

'She looks like a local, judge,' commented Bernal. 'Perhaps someone in Telde will recognize her.'

'I recognize her,' said the judge sadly, while Bernal looked at him in sudden surprise. 'I knew her long ago when she was a pretty young girl. Her name is Catalina Umiaga. She ran off with a travelling salesman, I recall.' He shook his head gravely over her bruised corpse, no doubt recalling her when she was sweet sixteen.

'What about the cause of death, Peláez?' Bernal asked.

'Lots of injuries to the face and head, Luis, that will take us time to examine and take cross-sections of. The skull may be fractured.' He helped the police surgeon to roll the cadaver over. 'Hullo, it looks as though her wrists and ankles were tied with a rope before death—there are clear hæmatoma there, but no cord now.'

'You'd better get her to the mortuary at Telde. I'll leave Lista and Gallardo here to liaise with the Civil Guard. I want to go to Arucas.'

After leaving Peláez at Telde, Bernal asked the police driver to take him first to the Gobierno Civil in Las Palmas. He thought it urgent to discuss the affair with the Civil and Military Governors. Miranda accompanied him to the meeting, while Elena helped Navarro co-ordinate the reports in their borrowed office.

The Military Governor received his civil colleague and the two detectives from Madrid with the utmost courtesy. 'It seems we have a crisis on our hands, gentlemen, with only a few days to go before the President of the Government arrives in Tenerife to start his tour.'

'Is there any news from there, Excellency?' asked Bernal. 'If as seems likely this is an inter-island independence movement, then something may be planned to take place there too.'

'Nothing so far, but the Civil Governor and the local police, together with Subcomisario Zurdo's team from Madrid, are keeping a close watch.'

'Then if the President is to be the target, it will be here on the eighteenth of July,' concluded Bernal. 'My view is that we must discover the new hide-out of these people and catch them before he arrives.'

'But we don't want any Press publicity,' said the Civil Governor somewhat nervously. 'Otherwise the Presidental visit might have to be curtailed.'

'I wonder whether the Civil Guard doesn't need the support of the army to search that difficult terrain to the south-east, sir,' said Bernal to the Military Governor. 'They also should have more air reconnaissance.'

'They've had one helicopter damaged already,' he replied crossly. 'We haven't got many on the island.'

'What about the latest infra-red and heat-sensitive detectors? Are any available?'

The Military Governor shook his head. 'We've nothing as sophisticated as that, Comisario. But we could try asking Madrid for it.'

'I should like a round-the-clock radio interception to be kept,' said Bernal. 'These terrorists must be in contact with their fellow conspirators on the other islands and possibly with North Africa where those four helicopters may have originated. With a constant radio watch and radar scanning we should be able to pinpoint their position.'

On the way out of Las Palmas, Bernal asked the driver to pull up at Consuelo's *chalé* where he went to talk to Manolita the maid. He found her seated at the kitchen table weeping inconsolably.

'What about the Señora's baby, Superintendent? Who'll look after her now?'

'I very much hope we shall find her soon. She must be quite strong to have escaped the way she did in order to telephone you. Unfortunately they caught her in the telephone-box. But she's resourceful; she'll try again.' He thought he was attempting to reassure himself as much as the maid.

As they drove on along the winding road westwards to Arucas, Bernal noticed that the landscape had changed, demonstrating the enormous variety of these islands. The villas with pretty gardens set among pines and eucalyptus-trees had given way to dense banana-plantations, in which labourers were weeding out poinsettias and other weeds and making large bonfires of them.

'Isn't it extraordinary?' said Bernal to Miranda. 'Those plants will be sold in the Peninsula for large sums at Christmas and here they're such a common weed they're being torn up and burned.'

The air seemed sharper and more rarefied in the hill town of Arucas, with its steep streets and uneven squares. They stopped by an impressive botanical garden and made their way to the police station. There Bernal inquired about the watch being kept on the home of the mysterious Señor Tomás, the registered tax-payer of the black Mercedes the terrorists had used, which was now in Civil Guard custody.

'There's been no movement at all,' the local inspector assured him. 'The house appears to be deserted.'

'But it's furnished?'

'Oh yes, though the neighbours say that no one's been there for three days or more.'

'I think we'd better get authority to break in and search it,' said Bernal. 'This is a matter of State security.'

When he rang Las Palmas, the Civil Governor was very helpful and contacted the local judge to ask him to issue the necessary order.

When Bernal, Miranda and the local inspector got to the pleasant-looking villa, set in a small walled garden, Miranda produced a set of *ganzúas* or skeleton-keys and set to work on the double lock in the front door.

'One of these is a security lock, chief. It will take some time.'

'Let's try the back. Builders always erroneously think it needs less protection.'

Miranda soon had the kitchen door open and they all went in. They noted that the refrigerator was well supplied with food as though someone expected to return soon. The pilot light of the butane gas hot-water heater was also alight. They found nothing out of the ordinary in the kitchen and Bernal made for the main living-room, which was expensively decorated and furnished. Bernal pointed to a writing-desk and asked Miranda to work on the lock. It presented no difficulties and Bernal was soon riffling through wads of papers, which included the car documents in the name of Juan Manuel Tomás.

'It's odd there are no photographs anywhere,' Bernal commented to the local inspector. 'Has Tomás no family?'

'The neighbours have said that no one lives here except him, Comisario. He has a girl in to clean the place twice a week, and a man to look after the garden from time to time.'

They noticed that the garage was built partly underground, adjoining the kitchen-door.

'Let's have a look inside, Miranda,' said Bernal, who was becoming used to his inspector's unfailing dexterity with the *ganzúas*. 'Where did you get those instruments, by the way?'

'From the Burglaries group in the Policía Nacional, chief,' he replied somewhat sheepishly. 'They said they'd never seen such a well-made set.'

They found the garage empty of vehicles, but they noticed a strong smell of kerosene.

'Why would anyone keep gas-oil in these quantities?' Bernal asked, looking at the rows of cans that lined the walls. 'It seems a dangerous thing to do.'

'There's a well-equipped workshop through here, chief,' Miranda called out. 'There are a number of shaped pieces of white matchwood on the bench.'

Bejnal picked up one of the pieces by its edge and examined it thoughtfully. 'We'll get Varga to run a comparison test.'

When they emerged once more into the garden, Bernal was still dissatisfied. 'There's something odd about this building,' he commented. 'Why is the garage sunk into the ground like this?'

'For the sake of appearance?' suggested the local inspector. 'The town-planners are keener than they used to be.'

'No, I don't think that's the reason for it,' said Bernal. 'See how the ground slopes away at the side of the house. That means there could be a hidden cellar between the garage and the kitchen.'

He went back into the garage and, getting a chisel from the work bench, began to tap on the inner wall at intervals along it. He stopped at a point where he perceived a hollow sound.

'We'll have to send for workmen with picks,' he said to the local inspector. 'There's a hidden chamber behind here.'

An hour later the workmen arrived and soon succeeded in making a breach in the single layer of breeze-blocks, revealing a large cavity which Bernal and Miranda inspected with torches. The large underground space contained fifty boxes of rifles with ammunition, and in a corner lay a very long wooden box without labels, with four smaller rectangular cases nearby.

'Let's get this open and see what else there is,' said Bernal to the local inspector.

The box was opened with a crowbar and they were astonished to find a portable missile-launcher, of Russian manufacture. The smaller cases proved to contain twelve SAM-2 missiles.

'They must have some radar equipment, chief,' commented Miranda, 'because this type of missile must be directed to the target by electronic means, but I don't see any here.'

'Make a thorough search,' Bernal told the local inspector, 'and we must arrange for all this matériel to be removed to a place of safety by the Civil Guard and the wall must be repaired and all signs of our visit obliterated. Then a discreet watch on the house may produce results when they return for these weapons.'

'I'll arrange for a furniture-van to be brought up to the garage-door, Comisario, so that the neighbours won't see what we're loading.'

'An excellent idea, Inspector. Look out also for any maps or documents here or in the house. We must find out exactly what they plan to do. In the meantime I'll inform the Military Governor of our discovery of this cache and I'll consult the Interior Minister in Madrid.'

Bernal contacted Navarro on the police-car radio to re-time the proposed conference for 1.0 p.m. and to invite the Military and Civil Governors to attend. 'I also want the Civil Guard lieutenant and his superior officer and Inspector Guedes from the Miller Bajo *comisaría* to be there too.'

When all his Group had assembled, together with the additional invitees, Bernal began by inviting the Civil Governor to preside.

'No, certainly not, Comisario. The Minister of the Interior has put you in charge of all matters concerning the security of the island during the Presidential visit. We shall be content to cooperate with you in every possible way.'

The Military Governor indicated his assent, but added: 'Any external threat to the eastern Canaries Province, that is to Gran Canaria, Lanzarote and Fuerteventura, falls under my direct authority from the JUJEM and the Ministry of Defence. But the President's security is your pigeon, Comisario.'

Bernal admired their political astuteness in placing all the responsibility on his shoulders should anything go seriously wrong.

'Very well, but this affair may be far-reaching and may include an external military threat to Gran Canaria from the Western Sahara. I suggest,' he continued, addressing the Military Governor, 'that all your forces be put on maximum alert immediately and that a full radio and radar watch be established to try and detect any suspicious movements by air or sea.' The Military Governor agreed to this. Bernal then turned to the chief of the Civil Guard and his lieutenant. 'The Guardia Civil is responsible for the security of the land areas and the coasts. The first question is: have you sufficient men to cover the fairly vast tracts that must be searched to find the terrorists' new camp?'

'I'm sure we have, Comisario,' said the somewhat indignant chief.

'We should expect results by this evening,' said Bernal firmly. 'If not, then your men must be supplemented tomorrow by army units.' Bernal now turned to the blue files in front of him on the table. 'The best piece of news is that we have seized the arms cache at Arucas, but its extent reveals the gravity of this conspiracy. The presence of a Russian-made missile-launcher shows that this is an international operation and not just a crazy plan dreamed up by a few local hotheads. Since we have only four days before the President arrives in the islands, we shall have to work fast to detain the ringleaders.'

'I've ordered the Policía Nacional to round up all those on our political files who might be involved, Comisario,' said the Civil Governor. 'We'll keep them incomunicado until the President's departure.'

'I recommend in the meantime that the guards be doubled on all public buildings and at the naval and airforce bases and army camps.' Bernal now opened the top file on the table. 'It will be helpful if we summarise the position and bring together our present knowledge of this group of terrorists and the means by which we stumbled on their operation, for "stumble" is the right word for it. When I arrived here I decided to peruse all the most recent police reports and I was struck by two cases that could be inter-related and that came within Inspector Guedes's competence. They seemed to be different from the run-of-the-mill type of case here. The man found drowned in Confital Bay on the morning of the seventh turned out to have been murdered. He had been hit a savage blow on the temple and then drowned in salt-free water, not sea-water. Dr Peláez has detected traces of kerosene and ferrous oxide in his respiratory tract. The second case was that of a woman found unconscious up at La Isleta near an abandoned hovel the same morning. She remains in a deep coma and has been unable to speak further other than the few words she uttered when first admitted to hospital. Is that correct, Inspector Guedes?'

'Yes, it is, Comisario. Rosario Pardilla's condition has deteriorated. The doctors don't expect her to last much longer. She's on a heart-lung machine.'

'Now tell me about her name, Guedes, since you haven't been able to track it down in any official file or in the electoral lists, have you? Did she give her name straight out as "Rosario Pardilla", or was it in a series of broken utterances?'

'It was a series of syllables, really. She kept asking for her husband, and it took her a lot of effort to give us her name.'

'I was puzzled about your inability to find her name on your civil files or at the Documento Nacional de Identidad, Guedes. Then it occurred to me, looking at this street-map, that near where she was found in the Calle de Coronel Rocha there is a side-street called Pardilla. Could she have been telling you her christian name, and then the name of the street where she lived?'

'That hadn't occurred to me, Comisario. I'll look into it at once.'

'And have you had any word from the Delegación de la ONCE, Guedes? The curious pairs of holes in the waistcoat-pocket of the deceased man reminded me of the clip-boards worn by the blind lottery-ticket sellers, and the physical characteristics of the victim suggest that he was an itinerant vendor.'

'They told me this morning that they're still checking, Comisario, but it's difficult because a few vendors work for a number of days and then don't turn up because of illness or other reasons.'

'I suggest you order your men to undertake a house-to-house inquiry in the Calle de Pardilla. It may be that there are no relatives who would report their absence, for it has occurred to me that the victims were man and wife. The woman was found clutching a sliver of wood from the blind man's stick and we found more pieces of it outside the hovel at Coronel Rocha. Now that hovel is of great interest and Varga and his assistant are going over it thoroughly this morning. It appears that an electric generator was installed there and a wireless aerial erected on the roof. The rusty oil-drum in the backyard containing stagnant water may be the place where the blind man was murdered.' Bernal turned from the files before him to look at his fascinated audience. 'Why should such a place be chosen, apart from its relative height above sea-level and its remoteness? After all, the high ground above Telde would be equally suitable if one wanted clandestine radio communication with North Africa or any of the other islands.'

None of those present offered an explanation.

'Then there is the case of Señora Lozano,' Bernal went on in worried tones. 'She is a high-ranking employee of the Banco Ibérico in Madrid and is temporarily seconded to the Las Palmas branch. The Señora is in the last month of pregnancy and what she did seems in retrospect to have been foolhardy. It happened that she discovered large monthly payments mysteriously transferred from Algiers in French francs to Paris and from there in pesetas to Las Palmas to the credit of a shady company called Alcorán S.A. The sums were drawn regularly by a Señor Tamarán whom she went to interview about certain serious irregularities in his companies' accounts two days after the incidents at La Isleta. It's now clear that she caused the conspirators to panic. They kidnapped her, probably at Gando airport that evening, and they're still holding her to the best of our knowledge. They abandoned the office they had rented in the Calle de Pío XII, leaving behind evidence that they had used radio installations there: one of the other tenants was incensed by the complex aerials placed on the *azotea* which prevented her from hanging out the clothes.' Bernal pulled out a letter from his pocket. 'In a search of the Alcorán offices, I came across the carbon copy of an express letter which at first seemed to be an innocent business letter, sent by Tamarán to a Señor Mencey in the Rue Lafayette in Algiers. It is written in French but the gist of it is that the trade basis had unexpectedly to be changed and the future coefficients for their profit calculations would be as follows until the eighteenth of July. Note the date. There are then set out a series of figures that are meaningless to me, but which I want the Cyphers Section to examine.' Bernal handed the letter to the Military Governor, who examined it with curiosity. 'Only last night did the name Mencey strike me as being of great importance, when Señora Lozano managed to escape and get a message to us about a "Mencey Plan" which seems to be an attempt to take over the island on the eighteenth of July.'

Navarro now intervened. 'I still don't see how we can establish a connection between the man and woman attacked at La Isleta and the abandonment of the offices in Pío XII by Alcorán S.A., chief?'

'There was nothing to connect them at first, Paco, except for the likely use of radio transmitters in each place. But when this morning we found the local woman, Catalina Umiaga, battered to death by Tamarán or his gang in the Caldera de los Marteles, I saw that the *modus operandi* was the same. Her body exhibited savage wounds to the head and had been thrown into the volcanic fissure, just as the blind man's corpse was thrown into the sea at Las Canteras. Then I asked myself why, if one had a transmitter in Pío XII, does one need another one in the heights of La Isleta? Inspector Guedes had pointed out to me the proximity up there of the main radio transmitters and receivers for official civil and military traffic and the coastguard station. That must mean that the illicit radio messages would be almost undetectable by ordinary surveillance and interception and would certainly be impossible to pinpoint, merging as they would with the legitimate wireless traffic. The site also offered a useful cover from which to attack and take over the main radio communications of the island when the time came. The other installations at Pío XII would pass as a normal commercial activity of an important company, and the plotters had to have back-up.'

'But are you seriously suggesting that a *coup d'état* is being planned for the eighteenth of July, Comisario?' asked the Civil Governor nervously. 'They would need immense military strength to overcome all our bases.'

'Would they, Excellency?' asked Bernal. 'Surely Lenin taught that a small well-organized band could take over an entire country if they secure all the key-points and the means of communication. It's much easier to bring about on an island that is only lightly defended. How many warships are in port at present, Excellency?' Bernal addressed the Military Governor.

'One frigate and two small assault ships,' muttered the official.

'And how many troops are in camp?'

'Most of them are national servicemen, and not fully trained. There can't be more than a thousand. The only experienced men are the legionaries, and their main base is in Fuerteventura.'

'So they would have to be flown in. How many military aircraft do you have?'

'Two Mystère jets, a transport and four helicopters.'

'You see!' said Bernal to the Civil Governor. 'Once captured, an island is very difficult to regain. I seem to recall that a proportion of five attackers to one defender is regarded as ideal by the military experts in order to take a well-defended island, while three to one is thought to be the minimum, and in this case there would be the enormous problem of putting the civilian population at risk.'

'But how could they provision and re-arm and refuel their force?' asked the Military Governor.

'First of all, we don't know how many other arms caches they have. But in any case if their seizure of power were to be successful, they would have all your supplies at their disposal. I suspect they will be counting on reinforcements from the Western Sahara. That's why I want you to order a constant patrol and radar scan of the African Sea. We must also put all the other six main islands in the archipelago on full alert. I expect they will try *coups de main* in all the capital towns.' Bernal turned again to the Military Governor. 'We must consult the JUJEM in Madrid to see what reserves can be sent from the Peninsula. I think we should ask for a parachute regiment and the GOE or Special Operations Group.'

The Governor gave his reluctant assent.

'Now we must do our best to arrest the mysterious Señor Tamarán,' concluded Bernal. 'The car documents we found in the house at Arucas show that the black Mercedes they used and which the Civil Guard are holding was in the name of a Juan Manuel Tomás. That could be Tamarán's real name, or another alias.'

'I've asked Inspector Ibáñez in Central Records in Madrid to check it out, *jefe*,' said Navarro, 'as well as all the records of separatist organizations here.'

'Good. What must still cause us enormous worry is that these plotters have all their radio equipment intact, four helicopters and at least thirty troops. If they are well-trained mercenaries they might succeed in taking over the strong-points, especially if they create a diversion so mind-boggling it would paralyze the authorities' responses.'

'But what could that possibly be, *jefe*?' asked Ángel.

'An attempt on the President's life,' replied Bernal grimly.

*

Throughout 11 and 12 July the Civil Guard, now reinforced by army units, combed the remoter areas of the south and the south-east of Gran Canaria without finding any trace of the terrorists. The radio interception station picked up no suspicious messages, while the constant radar scanning of the Atlantic and African maritime approaches revealed no air or sea traffic that could not be accounted for.

In deepest worry about Consuelo's whereabouts and physical state, Bernal sat glumly in his office in the Gobierno Civil at Las Palmas reading Dr Peláez's detailed reports on the autopsies. Inspector Guedes's house-to-house search in the Calle de Pardilla had produced results: one dwelling there was deserted, with the rotting remains of a watercress stew on a butane-gas stove that had long before gone out. A search of the sparsely and poorly furnished hovel had yielded only a rent book that revealed the name of the tenants as Gregorio Castillo González, a registered blind person, and his wife Rosario Méndez Baños. At least they could be interred together under their real identities, for Rosario, without regaining consciousness, during the early hours of 13 July had rejoined her husband in whatever part of heaven is reserved for those who have passed through this life without hope or help and have been dispatched from it as though they were no more than a casual nuisance.

At 7.30 a.m. on the same hot July morning, two amateur golfers who were staying with their families at the Oasis Hotel set out to play a full round of eighteen holes on the Maspalomas course before the sun rose too high and turned their game into an ordeal by fire. When they teed off at the tenth, one of them missed the fairway and his ball disappeared into the dry silt of the Barranco de Fataga which adjoins the course on the western side, near the low bridge over which the main southern highway crosses.

'At least you didn't hit any of the passing cars!' joked his opponent.

'Oh hell! You know how hard it is to get out of that dry river bed. I'll concede the hole.'

He scrambled off the artificial lushness of the frequently watered fairway down the rough bank into the silt and began to search for the lost ball. Just below the low road-bridge he caught sight of a colourful bundle lying in the dust.

'Something's fallen from the road. I'll take a look,' he called out to his companion.

'I hope it's not one of the foreign nudists who cross the course dressed only as on the day their mothers bore them.' said his companion, peering over the bank. 'They commonly take a short cut to get to the sand dunes at Maspalomas.'

'Perhaps it's a beautiful Scandinavian blonde just lying there waiting for me,' shouted back his opponent. 'You never know your luck.'

When he came up to the huddled form, his face turned pale when he thought he was looking at a bloodstained corpse.

'You'd better come down here. It looks as though there's been an accident.'

When Luis Bernal heard the news that Consuelo Lozano had been found dumped in the *barranco* near Maspalomas, his rage knew no bounds, and he decided to go at once with Elena Fernández to the Clínica de Nuestra Señora de la Paloma where the ambulance called by the Civil Guard had taken her.

In the well-equipped clinic he found she had been taken to an intensive care unit after her injuries had been assessed. The doctor in charge took Bernal to his private office.

'She's still unconscious, Superintendent, because of the blow delivered with a blunt instrument to her right occipital plane. I've run blood tests and started an immediate transfusion. The red-corpuscle count is very low, from the severe hæmorrhaging.'

'What about the child she was bearing, Doctor?'

'She's lost it, I'm sorry to have to tell you. And she'll

never be able to bear more children; the womb-damage is permanent.'

Bernal felt the white heat of anger grow in his head; the cold fear he had first experienced on hearing of the state in which Consuelo had been found was converted now into a thirst for vengeance. 'What's the outlook for her?'

'Reasonably good, I'd say, though these are early days. She's maintaining a steady respiration rate without mechanical assistance and a slow but regular pulse. She looks to have a strong constitution and with more transfusions to bring up her blood-count and intensive nursing she should pull through. It's too soon to say whether she'll have any amnesia from the blow on the head. The X-rays show no fracture of the cranium, but there is some bruising. The coma seems light and the encephalographic readings indicate a high level of cerebral activity. We're maintaining a saline and glucose drip and a constant check on the blood pressure and other vital signs.'

After thanking the doctor, Bernal went out to Elena and they both gazed through the glass panel at the ghastly pallor of Consuelo's face and her motionless form beneath the white sheet. Two masked and gowned nurses were tending her.

'Why don't you go back to the office, chief, and direct the search for these terrorists? I'll stay here and ask them to call me as soon as Señora Lozano comes round. She may have important information for us. Then I'll ring you at the Gobierno Civil.' Elena thought that her chief looked as pale as the terrorists' latest victim and needed to get away from the scene.

'Very well, Elena. But inform me at once, mind.'

Back at police headquarters Bernal and his team studied the large-scale map of the island with the Civil Guard lieutenant's assistance.

'The place where Señora Lozano was found is near this road junction where the Mogan road joins the main southern route from Playa de Inglés to Maspalomas lighthouse,' said the lieutenant. 'So our guess that the terrorists' new hide-out is somewhere in this south-east quadrant must be correct.'

'It's very strange that the Civil Guard haven't found them after all these days,' said Bernal. 'Nor has any illicit radio traffic been picked up from the area. They must have fresh vehicles available to them, or they couldn't have transported Señora Lozano in order to leave her for dead in the *barranco*. What is odd is that they should have brought her to a spot where it was likely she would be discovered quickly.' They didn't hesitate to strike down the blind man and his wife and Catalina Umiaga and dump them in remote places, so why did they relent in the case of Señora Lozano, who probably had learned far too much about their plans to be let loose? And they've lost the advantage of holding a hostage, so that, once we locate them, we can send in the GEOs without risking any innocent lives.'

'It could mean there's been a change in their leadership,' commented Navarro.

'Or straightforward panic when they found things starting to go wrong,' said Bernal, looking at the relief map. 'Now just east of where Señora Lozano was discovered there's a narrow road running up through Fataga to the Caldera de Tirajana. Wouldn't that large crater be a likely hiding-place, Lieutenant?'

'It would, but our men searched it thoroughly on the first day and there's no sign of them. We've combed the whole area on foot, including the section near the dams above Fataga.'

Bernal looked again on the map at the area west of Maspalomas. 'What is this radio station marked in the high ground above Pasito Blanco, Lieutenant?'

'That's a site leased by the Government to the American NASA Agency. They use it for tracking their space flights.'

'Have your men been there to search?'

'No, we wouldn't have interfered there. They have their own security people.'

'Still, it's interesting,' said Bernal thoughtfully. 'They make radio transmissions to Cape Canaveral presumably, which might act as cover for the terrorists' illicit wireless messages. I think we should ring up the NASA people and ask them if they've noticed anything abnormal.'

The lieutenant obtained the number and dialled it. They all waited with curiosity as he let the ringing tone continue. After two minutes had passed, he put the phone down. 'They're not answering this morning, Comisario.'

Bernal had a sudden premonition. 'Let's drive out there, Lieutenant, and take the commanding officer of the Special Operations Group sent from Madrid with us. There's more in this than meets the eye.'

Consuelo Lozano was slowly emerging from a terrifying dream in which she was tied hand and foot to a truckle-bed with her legs splayed wide, while the grotesque face of a Berber dressed in surgical white loomed over her as he drove a stake into her entrails. As she slowly regained consciousness, she could feel her arms pinioned and her legs too heavy to move. The strange loud buzzing noise had stopped and had been succeeded by a rhythmic bleeping. She struggled to open her eyes and made out a green television screen on which a series of lighter green waves passed from left to right. Suddenly she realized she was looking at a monitor of her own heart-beats.

Consuelo looked down at the transparent plastic tubes attached to either wrist and grasped that she was in a hospital bed. Thank God, she was safe at last. A soft female figure approached the bed and sat at her side.

'I'm Elena Fernández, one of Comisario Bernal's inspectors, Señora. The doctor says you're going to be all right.'

'And my baby? Is my baby safe?'

Elena shook her head sadly and Consuelo began to weep

quietly. After a while she said: 'Tell Luis about the device the terrorists have been trying out. It flies short distances and makes a loud buzzing noise.'

Bernal and the lieutenant instructed the police driver to take the approach road to the NASA station slowly, as though it was no more than a routine visit. At the large wire gate in the high fence two figures in brown uniforms carrying carbines could be seen.

'Are those the usual uniforms of the security guard here, Lieutenant?' asked Bernal. 'Those guards look like North Africans.'

'I've only been here once to consult the head of the station when we had a political kidnapping of an industrialist some time back, Comisario, and he let my men in to search the valley below the compound. The security men were from the United States and wore blue uniforms.'

'Get out and act naturally,' Bernal told him. 'Ask if we can talk to the commander of the station.'

Bernal watched anxiously as the Civil Guard lieutenant approached the gate, which the guards did not attempt to open. The GEO chief kept his pistol at the ready below the dashboard of the car. After a brief conversation, the lieutenant returned to the police car.

'They say there are none of the officials at the station, since there are no space flights in operation at present. They claim not to have seen any unusual activity.'

'What language did they speak?'

'Bad Castilian, with a strong foreign accent that seemed to be French rather than American English. They are North Africans, all right.'

Through the windscreen Bernal could see that the two guards had their fingers on the triggers of their carbines. 'Make a slow turn and leave as though everything's in order.'

The driver made a turn and departed at a slow pace. When

the gate of the station was out of sight, Bernal ordered the driver to stop.

'Let's have a look at your map, Lieutenant, to see if there's a vantage-point nearby from which we can overlook the station compound.'

'Just beyond the main buildings where the radar and radio tracking equipment is housed there's a gully that runs down to Maspalomas, Comisario.'

'Is there no high ground from where we could keep watch?'

'Only at El Tablero, but it's half a kilometre to the north-east as the crow flies. There's a narrow road leading up to the village.'

'Have you got binoculars?' asked Bernal.

The driver pointed to the glove-compartment. 'There's a pair of 30 × 70s in there, Comisario.'

'Good. Let's see what we can see from the highest point on the track leading up to El Tablero.'

When they reached the best point on the winding road, the three officers got out and took turns to sweep the area to the south-west with the powerful prismatics.

'There they are!' exclaimed the lieutenant. 'Those brown-painted machines in that clump of eucalyptus-trees in the *barranco*. They've not hidden them very well.'

'But they were banking on the Civil Guard not going into the US space station. They must be holding the American personnel prisoner if they haven't otherwise disposed of them,' commented Bernal grimly. 'How would you feel about organizing a raid on that site?' he asked the GEO chief.

'We need much more information about the terrain, the number of men the terrorists have and how they are disposed. Above all, we must try and figure out where the prisoners are being held.'

'Let's go back to Las Palmas,' said Bernal. 'You can plan it there with all the information we can obtain. In the meantime, Lieutenant, the Civil Guard must place a well-armed road-block on the track leading from the NASA station.'

'We could use artillery from here to destroy those choppers,' mused the GEO officer. 'We should have some aerial
reconnaissance first.'

'But they'd spot one of our helicopters at once,' objected
the lieutenant.

'We'll have to consult the Ministry in Madrid,' said
Bernal. 'This has now become an international incident, and
the Foreign Ministry will presumably want to consult the US
State Department. With the Americans' penchant for maxi-
mum publicity, we'll be lucky to keep any of this out of the
Press and that would make our task much more difficult.'

'Why can't we ask the Americans to give us high-level
surveillance, Comisario?' asked the GEO chief. 'They have
high-flying spy planes and satellites that could provide us
with very detailed photographs of the space station.'

'That's a clever idea,' said Bernal. 'I'll put it to our
Minister at once.'

Later in the day Consuelo Lozano began slowly to regain a
little of her strength and small signs of her usual optimism
from her brief chats with Elena Fernández, though she felt a
deep hurt and emptiness at the loss of her child from which
she thought she would never recover.

By evening the doctor decided she was well enough to be
moved out of the UVI into a private room. There she even
asked Elena for the loan of her make-up kit to make herself
more presentable for Bernal. When he arrived at 8.0 p.m.
bearing a large bunch of shining red anthuriums, Elena left
them alone as he embraced her.

Consuelo clutched Luis tightly and wept bitter tears while
he fought back his own.

'It's been hellish, Luchi, and those bastards caused me to
lose our child. I was half conscious when they manhandled
me into the helicopter and the contractions had started in
earnest. One of the Arabs held me down while another of
them tried to deliver our baby . . .' She broke into heavy

sobbing, and Luis tried to comfort her. 'But I knew . . . I knew it was dead before he handed it to me. It didn't cry or anything, and it was blue, Luchi . . .' She broke down once more. 'I knew when I was climbing up that mountainside that it had died . . . There was no more kicking or any sensation; just a dead weight inside me.'

Bernal kissed her while gripping her shoulders. He wondered whether the doctor had told Consuelo that she wouldn't be able to have any more children. Was it better to tell her straightaway or wait until she got stronger? And what had those bastards done with the stillborn's body? He hoped she wouldn't think about it. She looked him in the eye as though she had read his thoughts. 'And they threw it out when they saw it was dead, Luchi,' she sobbed bitterly, 'just like a rag doll. That's when I let go and passed out . . . I don't remember any more until we had landed and it was daylight again.' He squeezed her hands and began to weep openly. 'You know we won't have any children now, don't you?' Bernal nodded, unable to speak and saw her only through a blur of tears.

Consuelo, now racked with pity for him, sat up and tried to compose herself, as though demonstrating the greater inner toughness of her sex. 'You've got to get them, all of them, Luchi. Don't sit here wasting time.' She now felt a deep anger for the first time since her release, and Bernal thought it was perhaps a good sign.

'We've found the terrorists' new hide-out, Conchi, in the NASA station the Americans have got near Maspalomas, which these criminals have taken over. I've been in touch with Madrid and they've given clearance after consulting Washington for the GEOs to mount a major raid and free the NASA officials and security guards. We must capture these insane fanatics before the Presidential visit starts tomorrow at Tenerife.'

Consuelo remembered something very important she had to tell him. 'When the helicopter they took me in landed,

Luchi, I overheard Tamarán talking to his henchmen. They're trying to perfect a failproof assassination device which Tamarán was boasting would outwit all the security precautions anyone could provide.'

'Is it a missile-launcher of some kind? We captured one at their arms cache at Arucas.'

'I heard them trying it out at the crater where they first kept me prisoner and then in the new place I managed to crawl to a window to try and see what they were doing. That's when one of the Arabs caught me and hit me on the head. The device makes a strange loud buzzing noise. I don't think it's any kind of missile, though.' Consuelo suddenly remembered something else. 'What happened to the old woman, Luchi? The one who did the cooking for them in the crater?'

'We found her body in the volcanic fissure that had opened up there. She was a local woman from Telde, by name of Catalina Umiaga, who had had a very chequered career, according to the local judge.'

Tears rolled down Consuelo's face on hearing this. 'Poor old soul. She began to be kind to me, and in the end helped me to escape. That must be why those monsters did her to death. You must get them, Luchi.'

By the late morning of 14 July, Bernal had been in frequent contact with the Minister of the Interior in person, who was anxious that the President shouldn't leave Madrid until the security risk in Gran Canaria had been removed. Finally it had been agreed that, since Zurdo's team in Tenerife had uncovered no conspiracy there, the President would fly to Queen Sofía airport as arranged, but with modified schedules and changed times for his official functions in La Gomera and Tenerife itself. The decision was deferred as to whether he would continue the tour in the eastern Canaries province from 18 July.

The American Government had promptly provided excellent aerial photographs of the NASA station near Maspalomas, which were so detailed that the GEO chief could discern the four helicopters parked among the trees in the *barranco* and a number of vehicles outside the main building of the tracking station. The State Department had also transmitted copies of the ground plans of the station buildings and a list of the personnel. They had also agreed, unusually, to maintain a total Press blackout until the GEO operation had been mounted.

Bernal went over the plans for the raid with the commanding officer and the Military Governor. A regiment of parachutists had been flown out from Madrid and three extra units of the GEOs from Jerez de la Frontera and Cartagena. The plan consisted essentially of destroying the terrorists' helicopters with artillery at the same moment as the paras were dropped behind the fence of the station compound and the GEOs lowered on ropes from helicopters on to the roof of the tracking station. Stun grenades would be employed as these highly trained men smashed their way in at 4.0 a.m. on 15 July. In the meantime the Navy had despatched another frigate and the assault ship *Velasco* from Cadiz to reinforce the Las Palmas base and these were expected by the evening of the 15th, while the Fuerza Aérea had already sent four more Mystère jet fighters to Gando.

Thinking that little else could reasonably be done until the raid was undertaken, Bernal decided to spend the intervening time with Consuelo in the clinic to try and pull her out of the depression that had overcome her. He suggested plans for a summer holiday in the Peninsula.

'My brother has recently bought a splendid duplex apartment at Puerto de Cabo Pino, not far from Marbella, Luchi. He'd let us have it for a fortnight, I'm sure.'

'Ring him now, Conchi, and fix it up for us. It will save me from having to go to the annual village bull-run where Eugenia is expecting me.'

*

On the night of the GEOs' raid, Bernal took three of his inspectors, Ángel Gallardo, Juan Lista and Carlos Miranda, to Maspalomas where the GEO chief had set up his HQ at the Civil Guard post. There the lieutenant also awaited them.

'I'm going up to El Tablero to watch the artillery bombardment of the helicopters, Comisario,' he said. 'Would you care to accompany me?'

In the chill early hours of the 15th, Bernal and the lieutenant saw the mortars being placed in position and the aim being set on the half-hidden machines through the infra-red sights. At 3.55 a.m. they watched the transport planes approaching from the sea and then four helicopters arriving from Gando. At 4.0 a.m. precisely the signal was given over the walkie-talkies, and the mortars fired their first round with a deafening roar. The lieutenant tensely held a pair of night-glasses and suddenly chortled in jubilation.

'Two of the helicopters have been blown to bits and the third is on fire.'

'They must get them all,' said Bernal anxiously, 'or the ring-leaders may get away.'

A second round was fired, and there was a great flash and then a muffled explosion as the fourth machine was hit.

'They must have been refuelled,' commented the lieutenant, 'to explode like that.'

'They could have found suitable fuel at the tracking station.'

Further away, on the height, they saw the planes turn after dropping the paras and then small flashes from grenades as the Civil Guard helicopters hovered over the roofs of the main buildings. After half an hour the flashes stopped and the distant noise of small-arms fire died away.

'It's all over, Comisario. I think we could go over there now.'

They were met at the station gate by the triumphant GEO chief.

'We've got them all, Comisario, and we've found the Americans locked up in the basement of the building.'

'Any casualties?' asked Bernal.

'Two of my men have minor burns and one of the paras broke a leg on landing. We have complete control of the station. I'm waiting for a report on the number of terrorists killed or captured.'

By first light the whole camp had been searched and the wounded taken under guard for treatment at the military hospital.

'The total seems to be ten of the terrorists killed and six wounded,' the GEO officer told Bernal. 'There are six more who have given themselves up. We'll interrogate them shortly.'

'But there should be more of them,' said Bernal worriedly. 'Señora Lozano counted more than thirty in the crater at Los Marteles. Has Tamarán himself been captured?'

'Since we don't know what he looks like we can't be sure. All the documentation they carried on their persons is being examined.'

By noon on the 15th it was clear that not all the terrorists had been at the NASA station. Though he was most reluctant to ask her to do it, Bernal arranged for Consuelo to be taken in a wheelchair to the military prison and hospital for her to look at the prisoners and see if she could identify them, since she was the only one alive who had seen them at close quarters. She failed to spot Tamarán or his immediate henchmen among them.

'What about the ones who were killed, Luis? Perhaps they're among them.'

'I don't want to put you through such an ordeal, Conchi. You ought to be back in your hospital bed.'

'I've got to do it or you won't be able to proceed with the case properly. Now arrange to take me to the mortuary.'

Consuelo looked pale and shaken when the Civil Guard lieutenant wheeled her out of the refrigeration room.

'Tamarán's not there, but the Arab who struck me in the second camp they took me to is there.' She clutched Luis's arm and began to sob. 'You know, Luis, I felt an almost Germanic satisfaction when I looked on his face with the top of the head blown off.'

Luis comforted her and took her back to the car that had brought her. 'Now you go back and watch television and forget all this.'

Bernal consulted with the lieutenant. 'The ring-leaders must have left the NASA station soon after Señora Lozano was knocked unconscious. What I'm most concerned about is that we haven't found any trace of the assassination device they were experimenting with.'

'The GEOs are interrogating the captured men now, Comisario. I shouldn't think it will be long before they talk.'

'Check out each of the NASA officials' vehicles, Lieutenant. Tamarán and his close collaborators must have taken a vehicle.'

By the morning of 16 July, there was still no trace of Tamarán and his fellow conspirators, and none of the prisoners forcefully interrogated by the GEOs claimed to know where they had gone. Bernal obtained Photofit pictures from Consuelo's recollection of their appearance, and these were sent to all units. A car hired by one of the NASA officials at the tracking station was missing and still had not been traced.

On the evening of the 16th Bernal sat with the Civil and Military Governors going over the plans for the President's arrival the next afternoon.

'Perhaps we should urge him to cancel this part of his tour,' Bernal suggested. 'We can't ensure his safety with these madmen on the loose.'

'The President is anxious for the visit to go ahead,' said the Civil Governor. 'The General Election will be held in October and our party is keen to secure the Canaries seats in the Congress of Deputies.'

'But we still don't know what this assassination device consists of,' objected Bernal. 'How can we forestall it if we don't know what we're up against?'

'The presidential car is armour-plated, Comisario,' commented the Military Governor, 'and there will be sharp-shooters on the roofs all along the route.'

'I still don't like it,' said Bernal. 'We'll be playing for very high stakes.'

At lunch-time on the 17th, Ángel and Elena persuaded Bernal to take an apéritif with the rest of his group in the Plaza de Santa Catalina.

'You mustn't miss sitting for a while on the terrace of the Derby Bar, chief, and seeing the most typical sights,' said Ángel.

'This may be the last time I get the chance, Ángel, because I'll get the sack if anything happens to the President.'

In the warm sun filtered through the tall palm-trees they sat watching the daily parade of Africans selling false pearls, sharks'-teeth necklaces and figures carved in ebony; the portrait artist called Thea doing rapid sketches of tourists; and the Square's *pièce de résistance*, Lolita, who was rumoured to be the widow of an army officer and who appeared twice a day wearing different outrageously punk outfits with her face painted to match them, selling wrapped sweets and chewing-gum from an ancient Edward VII cigar-box and stopping from time to time to perform a brief dance for favoured clients.

'What an amazing sight this is,' said Bernal. 'I don't suppose there can be many places where you get the impression of all the races in the world going past.'

He spotted Varga crossing the square being pursued by persistent itinerant vendors.

'Varga, come and have a drink with us.'

'I was on my way to you with these reports on that pile of refuse up at La Isleta, chief. I think you ought to look particularly at the lab tests I've run on those pieces of light matchwood you found in the abandoned hovel which corr-espond exactly to the ones in the garage of Tomás's house at Arucas.'

'What are they, Varga?'

'That type of wood is commonly used for modelling, and the pieces found at Arucas were also varnished, as these small-scale models usually are. I think they are part of large model aeroplanes.'

'But what importance could these have? Perhaps it was Tomás's hobby?'

'I've been looking into the matter this morning, *jefe*.' He handed Bernal copies of three aircraft modelling magazines. 'Nowadays they can be made in fibreglass and various plastics, but the traditional and cheaper material is still matchwood. A small radio-controlled motor can fly such a model to a height of twenty-five metres or more, with a flight time of ten or fifteen minutes, depending on the fuel-tank capacity. They usually run on kerosene, and this is the important point, they can carry a load of two to three kilos, depending on the wing-span.'

Bernal flicked through the pages of one of the magazines and was surprised by the sophistication of some of the models depicted.

'So you are thinking along the lines of an explosive charge being placed in a model plane such as these and then its being controlled by radio to bring it towards the President during one of his official functions?'

'The possibility occurred to me, chief. When one thinks that it is quite difficult to kill someone travelling in an armour-plated car with bullet-proof windows, except by placing a large explosive charge under the roadway or by throwing a bomb at the vehicle, then this other means offers the advantage of surprise and of appearing innocuous until the last moment when it explodes. It also offers the terrorists the advantage of choosing the exact moment to produce the explosion and of easy escape, since they could be hidden some twenty or twenty-five metres away.'

'What does such a machine sound like in operation?'

'It makes a high-pitched buzzing from the small motor, which cannot be muffled. That's the only warning one would have until it came into sight, of course.'

'It would be very simple,' commented Bernal. 'But why would the terrorists have to try it out so often beforehand?'

'Because it needs a lot of expertise to control the model precisely with the hand-held radio, and the small motors frequently stall. It would be particularly difficult to operate in the dark.'

'How can we be sure that these pieces of wood are intended for such a purpose, Varga?' asked Lista.

'It's in my report. There are minute traces of nitro-glycerine on the samples found at La Isleta and at Arucas.'

Bernal took his inspectors back to the Gobierno Civil for an urgent conference with the provincial governors, the heads of the Policía Nacional and the Guardia Civil and the chief of the GEOs. He explained the technician's suspicions about the kind of assassination device that might be used.

'We shall search all the buildings lining the presidential routes, Comisario, and place extra sharpshooters on the high buildings. The streets will be lined with soldiers and police-men, whom we shall arm with rifles.'

'All of them must be told to shoot down any kind of model aeroplane on sight, or any other flying object,' warned Bernal. 'I gather that they can take curious forms, such as comets or even flying pigs, so long as the basic aeronautics are preserved. The speed of these models is relatively slow, between twenty-five and forty-five k.p.h., but they are set at a slower speed over longer dis-tances to conserve fuel. But since we've only found pieces of matchwood and no other materials we could perhaps assume that the terrorists will use traditional plane models.'

'What about the President's visit to the Parque Doramas tonight?' asked the Civil Governor worriedly. 'Can they be operated in the dark?'

'Varga says they could, but not with a good chance of success, especially not among trees.'

'I think we shall have to inform the President in person of the possible attempt on his life,' said the Governor. 'He will have to decide if he wants to accept the risk.'

'I agree,' said Bernal. 'In the meantime we must do everything possible to locate Tamarán and his henchmen. We've now got a photograph from the Documento Nacional de Identidad of the man called Tomás who may really be using the alias of Tamarán. That name, I've discovered from reading a history of the island, was the name for the aborigines' most powerful chieftain, while Alcorax or Alcorán was their highest god. The similarity with the Castilian name for the Kuran may be incidental, though appropriate in the circumstances. These names they chose confirm the fanatical separatist nature of the organization.'

'Does the photograph sent by Madrid resemble the Photofit done by Señora Lozano?' asked the Civil Governor.

'Yes,' said Bernal, 'though he appears much younger in the photo. It must be circulated to all units at once.'

Navarro came into the office with an urgent telex message. 'It's from Inspector Ibáñez in Central Records, chief. He's tracked down Tomás's connections with an extremist Canaries organization based in Algiers which had recently had contacts with the Polisario in the Western Sahara.'

By the afternoon of the 17th it was clear that the President would maintain his tour intact in spite of the threat to his life. Bernal decided to deploy his group at intervals along the routes, keeping in constant touch with them by radio. Varga's suggestion that the radio frequencies commonly used by model-aeroplane enthusiasts should be temporarily jammed found little favour, because of the risks of inadvertently jamming the police and security frequencies.

Bernal went to Gando in person to meet the President when he flew in from Tenerife during the late afternoon of the 17th, and travelled with the Civil Guard lieutenant in an unmarked car ahead of the official limousines.

'I can't imagine they could do anything when the President's car is moving at high speed,' said the lieutenant. 'The danger will be when the car slows at the turnings.'

'We must watch out for any attempt to halt the official parade, Lieutenant. They may try to block the road at the point they've chosen to make the attack.'

The whole presidential programme passed off without incident on the night of the 17th, and the maximum security in force at the Parque Doramas, although burdensome to those attending the banquet and reception and costly to the authorities, achieved its purpose.

Bernal was awakened in the Hotel Don Juan at 6.0 a.m. on 18 July by an urgent call from the Gobierno Civil.

'It's me, Paco, chief. Reports are coming in from the radar station of vessels setting out in a westerly direction from ports on the African coast some fifty kilometres south of El Aiaún. The Navy has despatched a frigate to investigate and a spotter plane has been sent from Gando. The radio interception personnel have monitored high-speed messages in code originating in La Isleta. These messages cannot be accounted for in the official or commercial traffic. They sent out detector vans to try and pinpoint the transmitter, but the broadcasts were too brief to track down precisely.'

'I always thought they'd choose today,' said Bernal. 'We must pull out all the security stops for the President's drive to open the new oil terminal at the Puerto de la Luz.'

Bernal again arranged his team along the route at the highest points, each of his inspectors accompanied by a marksman. He allocated the roof of the Hotel Don Juan to

Elena Fernández, then the roof of the main Post Office in the Calle de Albareda to Juan Lista, the top of the theatre at the corner of Juan Rejón to Angel Gallardo, the tower of the Castle of the Light to himself, and the tall warehouse in the Puerto de la Luz to Carlos Miranda, with Navarro coordinating the operation on their own radio frequency.

By 8.0 a.m. Bernal was installed with his marksman on the battlements of the Castle above the pleasant park in front of the Fishing Quay. The President's car was now due at 10.0 a.m. at the oil terminal, and Bernal chain-smoked Kaiser cigarettes as he looked from time to time through his binoculars for any suspicious movements. He watched far below him the groups of old men arriving after breakfast to throw their bowls in the sunshine and a group of children came to play hide-and-seek in the bushes.

The main Calle de Juan Rejón was lined with police and soldiers at twenty-metre intervals on each side, and at 9.45 the traffic would be stopped at all the road junctions. Bernal swept the fishing-port with his prismatics and could just make out Elena's slim figure far away on the height of the oddly shaped Hotel Don Juan building, appearing between the concrete pillars on the rooftop swimming-pool. The radio messages from Navarro began to keep him in touch with the President's progress. The official car had left the Calle de León y Castillo and had reached the Plaza de Santa Catalina without incident. Elena reported nothing suspicious as the parade passed her vantage-point.

The cars now picked up speed in the traffic-free Calle de Albareda, and Lista reported their progress across 'El Refugio'. A danger point would come, Bernal knew, at the theatre where Ángel kept watch, because the cars would have to slow down to turn into Juan Rejón. Suddenly Bernal heard a loud buzzing noise coming from the park below where he stood, and he craned over the battlements to see what was happening. A group of five small boys were starting up two large model aeroplanes on the grass near the quay.

He watched them with the utmost suspicion as they tried to get the motors to run smoothly, but they weren't accompanied by any adult and it all looked innocent enough. Bernal picked up his radio and called Navarro. 'Tell the police to go urgently to the Castle park and confiscate two model planes being operated by a group of children there.'

Bernal turned to see if he could catch sight of the official cars. The Calle de Juan Rejón was now empty of vehicles but he could see a truck speeding down one of the steep streets of La Isleta towards the main route leading to the oil terminal. He called again on the radio. 'Paco, warn the police that there's a large truck careering down the street opposite me.' He glanced at his street-map. 'It's called Artemi Semidan. Tell them to halt it before it reaches the Calle de Juan Rejón.'

The buzzing sound got louder and Bernal leant over the edge of the battlements. He could see four uniformed national police advancing rapidly through the flowerbeds towards the group of children near the fishing quay, but one of the model planes was now airborne, and the boys were trying to launch the second. Bernal was puzzled by the fact that none of them seemed to be holding the radio mechanism necessary to control the flight of the models. He was suddenly distracted by the sound of small-arms fire from the street opposite the Castle. The truck had burst through the police cordon and had come to rest across the main road, effectively blocking it for two-thirds of its width on the landward side. The official cars were only a hundred metres away and the leading police vehicle switched on its siren and swerved sharply on to the right-hand pavement to avoid the truck, the driver of which protruded through the broken windscreen with blood pouring from his head and chest. The police had stopped him, but too late, thought Bernal, his mind racing with anxiety at the speed of events.

He tapped the police marksman on the shoulder. 'Shoot down those model planes at once!'

The man had his finger on the trigger of his automatic rifle

with telescopic sights, and fired with admirably rapid reactions. The first model plane had reached the height of the
top of a palm tree near the edge of the road and as it exploded
with a huge yellow flash Bernal watched the palm-branches
disintegrate in what seemed like cinematographic slow
motion before the shock-wave knocked him to the ground
under the battlements. He got up dusting himself in time to
see the marksman take aim and hit the second model plane
which was just rising from the quayside as the débris of the
first was falling into the park.

The children ran for their lives and the four policemen and
the bowls-players lay face down in the dust among the *bochas*
just as the second explosion occurred, lifting a whole bed of
red and yellow cannas into the air and scattering them like
fine confetti bearing the national colours. Bernal felt less
blast from the second bomb and he peered over the edge to
see what had happened to the presidential car. The drivers of
the official limousines, as instructed, had swerved to avoid
the truck and then accelerated onwards to the gates of the oil
terminal, where they were now in safety.

Bernal congratulated the marksman and told him to keep
watch for anything else while he went down to investigate
and to report to the Civil Governor.

'Comisario!' shouted the marksman. 'There's a high-
speed launch leaving the fishing-port. It was hidden within
the first row of fishing vessels. Shall I try aiming at it?'

Bernal gave his authority, for he suddenly realized how
Tamarán had managed to be near enough to control the
flight of the model planes carrying the explosives, presumably by paying the children to start the motors while he
controlled their direction from the hidden launch. No
wonder the police and Civil Guard had been unable
to find him and his followers if they were holed up in a
launch, which would have given them the freedom of
movement along the coast from Maspalomas. On his radio
Bernal gave Navarro a brief account of what had occurred

and obtained confirmation of the President's safety.

He watched as the sharpshooter fired at the motor-launch which zigzagged as it sped out of the fishing-port into the wider part of the Puerto de la Luz and then past the Dique del Generalísimo, but the range was too great for him to hit the rapidly swerving target.

'I'll put out an alert to the naval base and the coastguards. He's bound to land somewhere on the island since he won't have enough fuel to reach Tenerife or Fuerteventura.'

By 11.0 p.m. word had come from the Navy that the Saharan naval vessels had turned back to their ports, but there was still no news that Tamarán had been sighted. The remainder of the President's engagements that day went off without incident, and the Head of Government proposed to continue with his tour of the eastern Canaries province.

At 4.0 a.m. on 19 July Bernal was awakened in his hotel room to be told of a small shipwreck at Punta Sardina on the north-west tip of Gran Canaria. A motor-launch had struck a reef at Roque Negro under the lighthouse that marked the entrance to the Puerto de Sardina. Three bodies had so far been recovered by the Guardia Civil.

Soon after breakfast Bernal collected Consuelo Lozano from the clinic, where the doctor had said she could leave to convalesce at home.

'I thought you'd like a morning trip across the north of the island to Puerto de Sardina, Conchi.'

'What a lovely idea. They have an annual festival there full of pagan rites, don't they?'

'I wasn't thinking quite of that,' said Bernal. 'I want you to identify Tamarán's corpse.'

THE END